THE FOURTH OF JULY

THE FOURTH OF JULY

{ *a novel* }

Kevin Dowd

Roundabout Press
West Hartford, Connecticut

roundabout ●

www.roundaboutpress.com

LCCN: 2012946347
ISBN: 978-0-98-588120-7

Illustrations by Kevin Dowd
Text Design by Libby Morris
Book Design by Sara Lewis and Libby Morris
Text set in Adobe Garamond
Printed in the United States of America

FIRST EDITION
9 8 7 6 5 4 3 2 1

ACKNOWLEDGMENTS

This manuscript was brought to life by the purpose and enthusiasm of the loosely-organized staff of Roundabout Press, including Dan Pope, Sara "Whitey" Lewis and Kristin Santa Maria (the Burnt Twig girls), Laura Hayden, Dave Holub, Michael Gilday and others. I'd also like to acknowledge the informal reviews and comments from people who read it in various forms over its eight-year gestation, including Bettina, Meg, Paula, Laurie, Laura, Joyce, Mary Kay, Mary, Marie, Evi, Danuta and possibly another Paula.

THE FOURTH OF JULY

PROLOGUE

{ LAURIE }

My name is Laurie Johnson. I was a volunteer with the island fire department. I was called to the Smith house the night it burned down. The fire was caused by gas from the neighbor's grill. The gas was on, but the grill wasn't lit. The two cottages were close together. Propane accumulated in the crawl space beneath the Smith house. Martha Smith was out front with the hose, watering flowers. After a few minutes, the artesian well pump under the house switched on.

The spark ignited the gas.

It was late in the evening on the Fourth of July. The island was overrun with drunken revelers. Some had pulled fire alarm boxes for the fun of it, so we had already responded to several false alarms. Worse yet, with fireworks going off everywhere, many didn't notice the sound of the explosion. The fire burned for fifteen minutes before we got to the scene. The Smith children were out at the time. Martha Smith was unhurt. Jack Smith was in the house, in bed. No one can explain how Jack escaped with only simple bruises.

When we rolled up onto the lawn, the front right wheel of the pumper broke through a septic tank, stranding the truck. I was in the passenger's seat, and as the vehicle lurched to a stop, my head hit a fire extinguisher mounted above the window. I bled a lot and still have a scar. The boys paid far too much attention to me, and not enough to the fire. In the end, we were no use at all. The house was consumed. We had barely pulled the truck out of the hole before the huge beech tree lit up.

In the morning light, debris littered the lawn. The cottage next door was singed, but remarkably intact. The burnt skeleton of a bicycle lay propped up against the remains of a tree. Mr. and Mrs. Smith sat on a blanket in front of the destroyed house through the afternoon. At sunset, they left with their children.

{ J A C K   S M I T H }

Wednesday, June 26th, 1974

All I wanted was a summer like those of my childhood: sand, salt water, swimming, sailing and fishing. No worries.

"Breakfast!" I hollered. The younger boy appeared in the kitchen, rubbing his ear. The older boy had fallen back to sleep. I climbed the stairs and tugged him from bed by a dangling arm. "Get up, get up!" I heard a disturbance from downstairs and dropped his arm to pay attention.

"Dad, someone's here," the younger boy shouted.

"Get out of your chair and see who it is," I muttered, stumbling back down the stairs. Useless kids. "I'm coming!"

I turned into the kitchen. "Jesus! What the hell is that?" I exclaimed. Janet's fat, middle-aged form blotted out the morning. Her screen-door shadow held the shadow of a cake—enormous in the backlight of the sun. I softened my demeanor to accommodate an uninvited neighbor bearing gifts.

"Nice to see you, Janet. How was your winter? Are your parents down for the summer?"

I stepped aside and pushed the door outward. Ample Janet swelled into the kitchen, displacing a precious volume of air. She pivoted about the cake. The cake gave her license. With her free arm, she smothered the younger boy at his breakfast—crushing him so that he dropped his spoon.

"Let me look at you," she said. "Oh, you're so big now. You should see the new playground. I heard that tennis lessons are—" Pretty soon, the boy stopped responding and she directed her fascination for bad news and conspiracy at me.

"You've got raccoons." She paused, expecting a reaction. "Somebody's got raccoons, anyway," she said, looking around the kitchen. "I saw them behind your house near the garbage cans."

I tried to choke her with silence, but could not restrain myself.

"How could we have raccoons? We've only just arrived. There isn't even any garbage."

"Maybe someone is putting garbage in your cans," she suggested.

"Perhaps you?" I muttered.

The older boy appeared, dragging his shoulder through the kitchen entryway.

"There's my other boyfriend," Janet chortled. She pulled him to her chest. The younger boy threw wadded paper at him, laughing. After a minute, she released the boy and returned to me.

"My folks will be down this weekend. They're bringing Grandma Lilly with them. She'll be ninety-five next week. My sister, her family, and my brother and his family will be here for the Fourth of July. We're having a big party."

I wondered how I could avoid attending. While Janet blathered about neighbors and the goings-on about town, I washed dishes to express my disdain for her gossip mongering. After a while she gave up, hugged the boys again, and wedged out the way she came.

"*That's it? A stupid cake?*" the boys asked. "*Where's the good stuff?*" She often fettered them with little trinkets—junk from Atlantic City, a postcard book or stink bombs. Sometimes they returned in kind. Last year they'd made earrings of the hard round lenses taken from fish eyes, though I doubt she knew what they were.

Summer, for me and the boys, was four days old. At the close of the school year, we'd escaped the suburbs in a car stacked to the roof with clothes, bedding and tools. The boys helped take off the shutters. We swept the linoleum and beat the rugs. The furniture belched dust into the stark sunlight. The floors and walls clung to winter, making the house feel chilly on a warm day. Last year's magazines looked comfortingly nostalgic. There was genuine reunion with forgotten toys; the boys fought over them as if they were new.

With the house open for the season, we ran down to the beach and dipped our white feet in the cold June waves.

"Who wants to make a sand fortress?" I asked.

"Nah," they said in unison.

"C'mon."

"Sand castles are for babies," said the younger boy.

"I said *fortress*."

One of them started to wander off.

"I'll be heading into town this afternoon," I declared. They turned to me with newfound interest.

"Where to?"

"To the lumber yard or general store—whichever has gray paint. We have to stop at the post office, too. We haven't cleaned out the box since last fall," I said.

"Can I get a new lure?" the older boy asked.

"Sure," I said, "if you help me paint the porch."

They agreed.

An hour later, I was preparing to leave for town when one of the boys' friends from last summer—a pudgy good-for-nothing—huffed up the hill.

"Dad, we're going down to the beach for a while," the older boy informed me. "Don't leave without us."

But they took so long, I went into town alone. We regrouped a few hours later, at dinnertime. After, the boys hurried out toward the shore again. Fighting to see past the setting sun, I stood on the front lawn scanning the beach, the docks and the marsh for any sign of their return. It was a beautiful view, and one I knew well. I'd spent summers on the island with my parents and siblings at our family cottage from childhood through my twenties. In my thirties, I rented summer weeks now and again with my wife, Martha, when she would come. Just before we separated, I bought a beautiful old Victorian on a hill.

I knew all of the old families. Martha made her own friends when she was there—mostly newcomers. She went out of her way not to befriend the people I knew; she refused to like them because I liked them. Between the two of us, though, we warmed up to enough friendships to exchange Christmas cards with the island's old guard and many of the new people.

Now, the musk of a skunk wafted up from the cool, darkening woods to the left. There came the snapping of thicket, followed by the boys' summer friend. He ignored my greeting and hurried home. My boys emerged through another hole, muddy but not skunky. I sent them to wash off in the outdoor shower behind the shed. I pulled up a lawn chair and returned to surveying the setting sun, happy to be back at the shore.

Hearing something behind me, I turned to find my childhood sweetheart, Chloe Truesdale, straddling her bicycle. Her three year-old bastard rode in a basket over the rear wheel. My first inclination was to flee. A hungry taproot extended from Chloe, searching for a man to provide for her and her illegitimate child. Touch her and she owned you. No number of unreturned letters could discourage her. When summer returned, she would inevitably arrive unannounced and ready to continue. I was always civil; she was still very pretty.

Chloe dismounted the bike. I sauntered over, showing calculated reserve and disaffection. She smiled warmly and leaned into me with a soft, aromatic boob-press. Her homunculus watched from the basket, looking bitterly jealous of his mother's affections. She began what turned out to be hours of chatter. She loosened the little mistake and pushed him toward my garden. After pulling a few strands of hair behind her ear, she untied her backpack.

"Oh," she said, rummaging through the pack, "I made a loaf of bread for you. I must have forgotten it. Well, I've got this," she beamed, extending an unlabeled half-bottle of wine.

Wine meant that she and the child were staying for a while. There might be alcohol-induced complications, too, as I had a tendency to take advantage of desperate, half-pickled women. To myself, I pledged restraint and good manners. All the same, I surveyed her form as I followed her toward the kitchen entrance. She noticed my interest in her backside and approved, giving it a little wiggle.

Before we reached the house, the boys ran out from the shower behind the shed wearing nothing but their underwear. They fell over one another trying to stop when they saw Chloe.

"Don't worry," she giggled. "I won't look."

That they were nearly naked wasn't the issue; they generally avoided any women callers, lest they run afoul of their mother and her mistrust of everyone. The boys sprinted in the other direction for the side entrance to the house. I could hear them bumping around upstairs when Chloe and I entered the kitchen.

"Would you like a little raspberry cake?" I asked, offering Janet's confection.

"These look like cranberries," she said.

"So, how are you?" I asked.

I'd hoped for a one-word answer. Instead, there was an atmosphere-consuming breath and a couple of tearful blinks. I learned that the bastard child's father had failed to provide child support. And that her mother had hooked up with a drunkard. I feigned disbelief as she described the difficulty she and the spawn had had securing social engagements on the island.

"So, do you prefer cranberries to raspberries?" I asked when she finally paused for a breath.

Thirty more minutes of laments passed until she realized that she hadn't seen her child for a while. Desperate for air—for any distraction—I jumped at the opportunity to look for him.

"I'll find him," I said, leaving her nervously clicking her heels at the kitchen table.

The screen door slammed behind me. I immediately forgot Chloe's little bastard. I stepped barefoot from the porch onto the wet evening grass. The sky was clear. The air was cool. Jupiter was big and bright. I could almost see her moons. I wished I had a cigar. I strolled near the garden and stopped to take in an unmistakable sound. The monster was peeing on a broad-leafed plant. I leaned in from the garden's edge and beckoned to him. The peeing stopped abruptly. Startled, he began to cry. I tiptoed timidly into the darkened garden, snuck behind a tall clump of sea grass, and snatched him from a steaming rhubarb patch. He screamed. Chloe flew out the kitchen door like a compressed spring, meeting us at the garden's edge, hands extended.

"What did you do to him?" she demanded.

"What did I do? I guess I scared him."

"Father Ivan says when he screams like that, he's seen the devil."

The kid's pants were still down about his knees. His business was hanging out. She snatched him from me, re-fastened his fly and clutched him close, babbling comfort in his ear. He blubbered on her shoulder, dragging his snotty nose off long enough to glare at me and begin crying again. The tense moment passed without further word and her former demeanor returned. There was more chitchat in the kitchen over the dishes in the sink. I offered Chloe an aperitif but she declined. Thinking I might get a little something, I offered her the front room for the night and she declined again. I cupped her ass.

"We have to be going," she said.

"But it's very late."

"We'll be fine," she insisted.

The dew had soaked the bicycle and basket. She wrapped her now sleeping ball 'n chain in my coat, mounted the cold wet seat, and pedaled shakily across the soaking grass, out to the road and down the hill. The bicycle's rear fender rattled in the darkness.

Thursday, June 27th

A zephyr kissed me through the screen of my bedroom porch door. I propped myself up. Through the morning haze, I could see a ferry approach over the glassy bay. Three women stood on the crib dock, dressed in white, wearing sun hats. They'd be boarding the return boat for the market in New London. The men of their houses would be glad to be rid of them for the day. However, the time it took to get to the market made rash purchases likely, and these men would have to pay for them once in cash, and then again as they listened to the rationale behind the purchases. If they objected, they'd pay a third time in the bedroom.

Downstairs, I searched for coffee pot parts in a sink full of standing water. The remains of the boys' breakfast lay on the table. Sunshine beamed through the half-open door, suggesting which way they had gone. I abandoned the sink and followed them. I passed through the rose trellis and out into the open sunlight. I sucked in a chest full of morning air, first refreshing, and then reeking of trash.

As I turned the corner by the shed, I found my trashcans toppled. The ground was littered with onions, bones, egg shells, flour, fruit, and fashion magazines—none of these from my house. "What's this all about?" I demanded of the trash. I righted a barrel and called out the boys' names, frustrated that they hadn't taken some responsibility and picked up the mess. There was no answer. I kicked through the refuse and continued on my way to the shed. It was time to put the boys to work. I'd take them to the boatyard and make them help prepare the boat for launching.

Paint, I said to myself. *We need boat paint.* I extracted paint cans from the spider webs at the back of the shed. The cans weighed nothing; the paint within them was dry. I would need paint, new brushes, oakum and seam compound to ready the boat.

"Boys?" I yelled out.

My voice resonated through the empty can. I gathered some rags and a scraper into a peach basket and headed back toward the house, taking the other way around the shed to avoid the trash. I dropped the basket on the bench by the trellis and returned to the kitchen.

"Boys!"

Still, no answer. I dumped coffee grounds into the percolator, having never found the filter basket. Sitting on the bench under the trellis, I waited for the brew to finish.

Ants are amazing, I thought, looking down. Some searched. Some dug. They crossed every which way, stopping to rub antennae, should they meet. What did they tell each other? They seemed so insignificant by themselves, but taken together they owned the world. I bet they knew all the goings-on across the island. I watched a pair of ants drag a writhing worm toward their hole.

I flicked an ant from my calf, pushed off the bench and returned to the kitchen for the coffee. I wrote a curt note to the missing boys, adamant that they help me prepare the boat. I spilled gritty hot coffee into a carafe and set it in the peach basket full of rags. I had my head in the trunk of the car when our parish priest, Father Ivan, pulled up in a sedan. I straightened up, inconvenienced—waiting as he took too long getting out of his car. He closed the few steps between us and extended a chalky hand.

"Hello, Jack. How is your family? How is your dear aunt?" He continued before I could answer: "I saw Chloe Truesdale this morning. She stopped by with a loaf of bread. Her darling little boy was with her."

"They were here last night," I said quickly, pushing the conversation along.

He continued as though I hadn't spoken. "She mentioned that they visited with you last night. I told Chloe how your family and I go way back—your parents and aunt and all. Chloe comes to help out at the church sometimes. You have two boys. They might like to help out around the church. They could be altar boys, or come swimming at the lake. Chloe's boy spends time with me at the lake."

He rambled on without working toward a point. In the distance, across the yard, Janet's broad form took up a position over Father Ivan's shoulder, eavesdropping from her side of the fence. She could hear but every other word. She would invent the rest. I was angry about the garbage, for which I squarely blamed her. And here she couldn't even mind her own business.

"What do you *want?*" I boomed.

Father Ivan sucked in a breath and popped out his eyes. "I'm looking out for the well-being of the boys!" he thundered back. Janet ran away.

Father Ivan thought my outburst was about him. I should have apologized instantly. Instead, I sorted through what I had just heard him say. *Was Father Ivan talking about Chloe's boy? My boys?* He had no business looking out for my boys. But I didn't want to cross him. Priests, like policemen, are capricious instruments of damning authority. The most important thing at the moment was to cool him down. I fumbled for words.

"Father, I—I'm sorry. I wasn't talking to you. I was—won't you come in?"

I was raised to respect priests. It took some time and pandering for me to convince him that my anger was about garbage and not directed at him. We sat in the living room making nice, drinking tea and listening to the clock. I made my penance by volunteering for some unspecified future church activities. I never came to understand his motives; all that mattered was that he eventually left.

I couldn't find the boys that morning and went to the boatyard alone. My car bounced into the dirt lot where the boats sat in cradles. I looked into the peach basket. There were mouse droppings in the oakum and my brushes were chisels of hardened paint. In my head, I listed the supplies I needed. I pushed the coffee carafe aside. In hell, the coffee is always hot. But thanks to the priest, mine was cold. I continued down to the boatyard store for supplies.

"Got any coffee?" I asked loudly with cup in hand, entering the shop.

A figure stooped over the pot. Hearing me, he rose up to his full height. "Good Lord," I said, wondering how Father Ivan had beaten me here. But it was Father Ivan's brother, Captain Bob—not dissimilar in appearance. Before Captain Bob could answer, the proprietor appeared from the storeroom.

"Sure. Help yourself."

He pointed to Captain Bob.

"How do you do?" asked Captain Bob.

It was as if I were being offered a cup of Bob.

Bob's full name is Robert Malinowski. That doesn't conjure the old salt he fancies himself to be, so he goes by "Cap'n Bob." I referred to him as "Phony McPipe" because of the corncob and the tall stories I'd overheard. The Panama Canal was his idea. He claimed that he was aboard the *Endeavor*. He could bore a man to death. Like a child who has witnessed another having a splinter removed, I never wanted to be next, which seemed unavoidable now.

"How are you, Cap'n Bob?"

With a fixed grin, he rode his uncertain, spidery-thin legs over to where I held my grounds.

"I don't believe we've met," he said, weighing his prey.

"Sure we have. I'm George Smith's son," I said, examining the resemblance to his priestly brother.

"Oh! How is George?"

"Well, I'm afraid he—"

"Tell him I said hello. You know, George and I once took a boat to Montauk and—"

And, and, and. He went on for twenty minutes. But unlike the time spent with Father Ivan, he was at least telling me something interesting: stories of my dad. I was suddenly taken with Cap'n Bob.

"We'll have to share a drink at the club. Very nice meeting you," he said.

"That sounds good. Nice to talk you too, Cap'n McPipe," I said genuinely.

He strode off. I discarded my cold coffee and looked for the supplies. I bought a can of red copper bottom paint, dark blue topside paint, white paint for the boot stripe, oakum for the seams, seam compound and sandpaper. I re-crossed the boat lot in the late morning sun and removed the canvas tarp from the cradled boat. The rest of the day I scraped, sanded and caulked. Layers of previous years' colors sanded to different depths gave the boat the look of an aggie. The new paint would have to wait for another day; time grew late. I returned the basket to the shed when I got home.

The boys lay crosswise on the living room furniture. Their clothes were dry but their hair was full of salt.

"Where were you today?" I asked.

"I thought we were going to the boatyard with you," said the younger boy, sounding a bit irritated.

"You disappeared."

"We were at the beach. Why didn't you come looking for us?" he asked.

He was right. I could have looked for them at the beach. Though, I could have just as likely driven all over town looking for them.

"Did you eat?" I asked.

"We caught some fish."

"Oh, great. Do you want me to cook it?"

"Nah, we already ate."

They'd eaten toast, not fish. The crumbs left by the toast, the butter and the plates remained out in the kitchen. I was starving. The stark, uncleaned blackfish in the bucket looked appetizing. At the same time, I was sunburned and lethargic from my long hours working in the boatyard. So, I too made some toast and returned to the living room to eat it on the coach.

"Nice catch. What did you use for bait?"

"Lures," said the older boy.

"I thought you didn't have any."

"We made them from old keys."

"Really? And that worked?"

"Yeah, they're great."

"So, who will go with me tomorrow?"

"Where?" they both asked.

"To the boatyard. We have to paint the boat."

"Oh, I love to paint," said the younger.

"Me too," said the older.

I fell into bed at sunset, coated in cold cream and drained by worsening sunburn. I was drifting off to the lullaby of the waves until it was accompanied by the timpani of garbage cans. I threw off the sheet and stumbled to the back window. It was dark, but I could just make out a black creature with a white stripe, waddling around the corner.

Friday, June 28th

The next morning, I took an early stroll down to the post office, the crib dock, and then over to the Crescent Club. It was just me and a steward named Mike. He was chasing a cigar butt off the concrete with a garden hose.

"Morning," he said.

"Good morning. What's all this?" I tipped my head toward some provisions under tarps.

"Tables and chairs. Clam bake tomorrow night."

"Oh yeah," I said, reminded. "Too late to sign up?"

"I dunno." He pointed toward the glass case where the bulletins were kept. I pulled the wooden peg securing the door, swung the glass open and penciled in a reservation for two under my name.

I waded along the beach, turning over a few rocks. The bay was afire with reflections like diamonds in the morning glare. The sun's rays taunted my sunburn. I retreated up the hill to find shelter at home.

At breakfast I told the boys: "I'm going to send you two to paint alone today. I'm too sunburned."

"Okay," they said in unison.

I sat in the car, watching the morning ferry, waiting for the boys. I cranked the engine when they approached.

"Got everything? Got the paint?"

"Oh, yeah," the older one said and ran off to the shed. He returned with the peach basket and set it in the trunk.

"Got brushes? Rags? Turpentine?"

"Yep. It's all in the basket."

I dropped the boys at the boatyard. They would have the whole day. I suggested that they try for two coats of paint.

Back home, I made a pot of coffee. The fish had ripened overnight in the sink. I wrapped it, took it out to the garbage cans and cleaned up last night's mess. I pulled a rocking chair from the porch wall, taking generations of spider webs with it. With my feet on the railing, I rocked gently and watched the activity in the bay. The midday ferry was arriving. A driver stood onboard by his delivery truck and two shapely women climbed into a convertible, ready to disembark. I jumped up for a pair of binoculars, eager to see who they might be. Nobody I knew; day tourists. I thought it might be fun to look for them in town later, when they were having drinks.

I'd invited a few people to come visit over the next several weeks, but none within the timeframe of the clam bake tomorrow night. I considered the locals. If I asked Chloe, she'd take it as a marriage proposal. Janet was too fat. I hadn't spoken with another local friend, Elizabeth, yet that summer, and thought I might leave it that way for the time being. I had reserved two spots at the clambake, but I didn't care to pay for an empty place. Driven by frugal second-thoughts, I launched myself from the rocking chair, stepped off the porch and made my way down the walkway under the shade of the beech tree and out into the sunshine of the street. I entered the road a few steps ahead of a girl making her way down the hill. I guessed she might be in her late teens; I wasn't familiar with her. I nodded *hello*, but said nothing—not expecting a return greeting.

"Hi," she said from behind me, a little too far away for conversation.

I turned and said "Hello," over my shoulder, and continued walking.

"I like your house."

I stopped to let her catch up. "Thanks," I said.

"I think you're cute too," she volunteered. "I'm Allison."

I'm sure I blushed. How else could I have responded?

"Oh, thank you. Nice to meet you. You're cute too. I mean—my name's—"

"Jack," she interrupted. "I know all about you."

"I, uh—," I started, but she cut me off again.

"I live up the street. Will you show me your house sometime?"

"Uh, sure."

"I'll show you mine," she said.

"Um, okay."

She turned left up the road towards the post office. I continued on to the Crescent Club. That was odd, I thought to myself. I replayed the scene in my head. It seemed like she was coming onto me, a forty-something year-old man. I reached the sign-up sheet for the clambake and scratched the *2* from next to my name. I peeked into the clubhouse and entered to read the main bulletin board.

"Join me for that drink?"

Cap'n Bob was seated at a table, alone. He held a bottle of rum up at me as if it were a prize. I didn't want anything to drink at ten-thirty in the morning, but Cap'n Bob was my new friend and the de facto center of attention in the empty clubhouse. I couldn't just walk away.

"Well, I guess one wouldn't hurt," I said.

Today's conversation was not like yesterday's; Phony McPipe ran on about everything and nothing. I found myself desperately far away. Occasionally, a change in his tone or manner would tug me back, but I had no idea what I was nodding agreement to. My bored hands and lips sipped at glasses of rum, one after another. My head swam worse from the sunburn. At one point, McPipe stood up and went to the lavatory. I concentrated cross-eyed on his return, unable to gauge the time. I waited, alone with the bottle of rum, sipping. McPipe never came back. The restroom had a back door that leads out through the bathhouse. He might have dismissed himself and I might have missed it.

Without warning, the ladies' Friday noontime bridge league blossomed into the clubhouse. They wore airy dresses and bonnets. They twittered and laughed. They were agents of virtue, temperance and matronliness. I was red-faced and cross-eyed. The rum was fresh on my breath. A half-emptied bottle stood on the table. They consulted together. The lead hen walked over.

"Do you mind if we use this table for bridge? You could find a spot for yourself over there." She pointed to the closed bar.

"That's one of the Smiths, isn't it?" I overheard, coming from the gaggle.

"Of course you may have the table," I said as brightly as possible. But I'd been sitting with Phony McPipe so long that my legs were stiff. I stumbled. A woman's voice exclaimed: "Oh!" Another fetched a steward to help me. I was not in the tipsy condition they believed me to be in, but there was no redeeming myself. I said, "Good day," to nobody in particular and headed for the door.

"You forgot your bottle," said one woman.

I lumbered up the hill in the bleaching sunlight. I was hungry. The boys had left the makings of a peanut butter and jelly sandwich out. I smeared peanut butter on a slice of bread. When I opened the jelly lid, ants erupted as if I'd popped off the top of Vesuvius. "Ach!" I exclaimed, dancing backward from the counter. Everything went into the garbage and out to the cans. I abandoned any thought of lunch and collapsed on the living room sofa.

Early evening. My head ached. I'd forgotten the boys.

I left a cloud of dust on my way into town. I skidded to slow for an oncoming patrol car. The boys were in the backseat. I turned around and gingerly followed them home. When I arrived, they were thanking the constable for the ride.

"That your father?" I heard him say.

"Yes, officer."

He walked over. "I'm Constable Howard," he said. I already knew who he was. He already knew who I was.

"Thank you for bringing them home, Constable."

"I'm looking out for the wellbeing of the boys," he said. There was an awkward silence as he took a hard look at me. Then he left.

I turned to the boys. "How did the painting go? Why aren't you covered with paint?"

"We had plenty of time to clean up," the older boy said.

The younger kicked some dirt and wandered off.

"Thanks for leaving us there," he muttered.

Saturday, June 29th

The roiled hissing and screeching of animals fighting over scraps from the trashcans could have awakened a sleeping drunkard. At about eleven, a skunk sprayed one of its dinner mates. The odor drove us all into the living room for the remainder of the night.

Sunken-eyed, I surveyed the scene at dawn. There was refuse everywhere, some of which I didn't recognize. Garbage ferment, egg wash and jelly had soaked into the earth, making it shiny and interesting to flies. I looked up and my gaze met the red eyes of my next-door neighbor Frank, Janet's father.

"You've got to secure these cans," he groaned. Frank didn't say anything else—not *How are you?* or *How was the winter?* He simply walked back to his cottage.

"I thought I had secured them," I mumbled to myself. In fact, I'd tied the lids with cords. I left the mess as it was and returned to bed. The boys and I awoke a second time for a late breakfast. We had butter sandwiches and stale cranberry cake.

"We need groceries," I said.

I took the boys into town with me. I was picking over the fruit in front of the village market when I came shoulder to shoulder with the widow who lived a couple of doors up the street from us, Mrs. Steeves.

"How's Martha?" she asked.

"Martha and I, well, we're separated. How are you?"

"Oh dear, that's a shame. She's a lovely girl. How are those poor boys getting along?"

"Well, they're fine. In fact they're right over there." I pointed to two hellions pitching melons at each other like barques exchanging cannon fire. I raised a palm to hold back the gush of Mrs. Steeves' small talk.

"Put those down!" I hollered.

Mrs. Steeves spoke through my hand. "Martha took good care of me when I fell. My shoulder is almost back to the way it was, except when it rains. Oh, we had a dreadful spring. Have you met my grand niece, Allison?" She pulled a teenage girl forward by the arm.

"If you need anything, you just ask," I offered, ignoring her as I abandoned the conversation to break up the boys. Glancing back, I was astonished to see that the niece was the girl I'd spoken with in the street the day before. She gave a smile and a little wave. When she was sure that her aunt wasn't looking, she blew me a kiss.

"Damn!" I exclaimed on the ride home. "I meant to swing by the boatyard. Do you think the boat is ready to go in water?"

Both boys agreed that it was. We stopped at the shoreline post office where I used the telephone to call the boatyard.

"Hello, this is—," the proprietor recognized my voice and cut me off. He agreed to have a look at my boat to see if she was ready.

"Set the mooring off the Crescent Club. If there's a problem, let me know. We'll be racing, so I need her for the weekend," I said.

The boys ran off as soon as we pulled up to the cottage. I stood on the porch looking at the lawn and then beyond to the water. I stepped into the kitchen and checked the kitchen freezer for one of my boyhood treats, a Popsicle. I shuffled out to the porch, unwrapping a green one. Staring at the bay, I tested the frost on the Popsicle until the flavor blossomed.

"This is awful."

I tossed the Popsicle over the porch railing, into the bushes. I turned to the right, surprised to find someone standing near me in the shade on the front lawn. It was Allison.

"Didn't like your Popsicle, huh? I brought you some cranberry cake," she said, giggling.

I couldn't come up with a response. Allison stepped up on the porch with a wax paper-wrapped plate. As she closed the distance between us, I held out my hand for the cake. Her free hand found my waist and she stood up on tiptoes to kiss my cheek. Entranced, I lowered my head to look at her. She kissed me again, this time on the lips. I tried to speak as her hand slid up from my waist to the back of my head. She pressed my lips into hers for what turned into a long and ultimately open-mouthed kiss.

"Mmmm. Lime," she whispered.

She felt, smelled and tasted wonderful. It was so strange, though. *Who was this girl? How old was she? Why me?* She didn't give me the opportunity to ask. She set the cake on the arm of a chair, turned and sashayed down the walkway toward the gate and out into the street. I looked after her for a few moments, touched my fingers to my lips and then went back into the freezer for another green Popsicle.

Twenty minutes later, I stood in front of the Crescent Club. The stewards raked wood chips and trimmed bushes. A group labored under the dinner tent. The food committee had already erected tables and chairs, set up boilers for corn and lobsters, and laid out serving stations. I offered my help.

A clambake starts with a rock-lined pit. One starts a large wood fire, allows it to burn to coals and then smothers it with seaweed to make steam. The clams are thrown onto the steaming seaweed and buried under more seaweed and a canvas cover. Our pit was incomplete, though, and time was running short. Two men dug desperately. I forked wheelbarrows of seaweed gathered by beach kids. We switched off periodically. Passers-by stopped to say *hello*. By early afternoon, our seaweed mound ripened in the sun, gathering flies. People gathered, too. I finessed the hole. The silhouetted head of yet another visitor cast a shadow into the pit and spoke from the corona.

"You're digging quite a deep hole."

It was Elizabeth, one of my longtime female friends. I clambered out and gave her a sandy hug in the cloud of swirling flies. She backed away and brushed off the sand.

"You're a mess," she said.

"Are you coming this evening?"

"I'll be with my aunt and some of her bridge club friends. You're welcome to join us."

I said that I would.

On the way home, at the foot of the hill, I caught my first yearly glimpse of Lilly, Janet's grandmother. Lilly was an ancient, wrinkled, walking non sequitur—a collection of unsolicited facts about forgotten things. I was always surprised to see her return in the summer; sure that winter's icy fingers would cull her and spare me the idle chitchat. But death cannot take itself, I suppose.

When I drew near, she began rambling spontaneously: "You know, you should water your plants in the evening."

"Hello, Lilly. How are you?" I said, trying to circumvent her nonsense.

"Oh, I'm old," she replied. "But you shouldn't water during the day. The drops will burn the leaves in the sunshine, and the roots don't have time to soak up the water."

I considered that it rained much of the week before we got here. I could wait another week before watering anything. "I can't water flowers, Lilly," I said, "I have an iron leg bone and I'm afraid it might rust. But if you want to, the garden hose is right there. Just don't drain the well dry."

"Well," she trailed off, "I guess so."

I tugged a summer suit from the closet, pomaded my hair and donned an antique straw hat.

"Alright," I said to the boys, "I'll be back to check on you at nine o'clock. I want you to stay in for the night. Okay?"

I marched down the hill to the Crescent Club and joined an early group gathered on the beach beyond the tents in the bright summer evening sun, rum punches in hand.

Roger, a fellow boat owner, passed me the punch ladle.

"Are you going to race this year?" he asked.

"Absolutely. I've already cleared a place for the cup," I said. "Is your boat in the water yet?"

"She's going in this week—in time for the Fourth of July series. How about you?"

"Any day now," I said. "I heard Foster bought a new boat."

"Maybe that's it," Roger said, chuckling and gesturing with his glass toward an entirely gray boat out in the mooring field. "It looks like a battleship."

"That's hideous," I said. "Speaking of sailing, I need a steady crew. Got any suggestions?"

"Well, you can't have mine," he said. "Crew is getting harder to find. We're up to twenty boats."

"Twenty, really? That's terrific."

The fleet had doubled in a year; racing was the latest club craze. These older wooden boats, called *Zips*, were small and affordable enough for every household, but seaworthy enough to race in heavy weather. A Zip required a two- or three-person crew for racing.

One of the older club members, Mrs. Peterson, joined us with drink in hand. She was beaming. "I heard you're helping Father Ivan with the festivities."

"I'm what?" I asked.

Roger slunk away.

"Helping with the church picnic at the lake. That's just wonderful," she said. "We're having a planning meeting after morning Mass tomorrow. In the rectory."

I hadn't volunteered for anything. Father Ivan was taking cart blanche of my time. I resolved to skirt it. I cut Mrs. Peterson off, feigning a connection with someone across the way. Then, as requital, Chloe appeared in the very spot. Her suckling bastard followed, battling its way through the adult legs of this adults-only gathering. Helpless with a glass of punch in one hand and stuffed mushroom in the other, I got hugged. Mrs. Peterson's smile soured at the spectacle, and her empty glass tugged her back to the bar for a purgative. Waiters wandered through the crowd with scallops wrapped in bacon. Over Chloe's shoulder I saw Elizabeth chatting with Roger.

"I'm sorry about the other night," Chloe began. "I talked to father Ivan. He said it was okay. I didn't know that you two were such good friends."

"What about the other night? What did Father Ivan say? I hardly know the man."

As Chloe was about to explain, her monster fell on the concrete breakwater, letting out a mortal scream and bloodying his knee. Chloe rushed off. A couple of members of the bridge club slid by me. One of my mother's old friends tramped over. There was no greeting.

"Have the boys seen their mother?" she demanded.

"Yes, of course. Just before we left Hartford," I said.

"I don't know why you two split up," she said. "Martha is such a sweet girl."

I could not begin to explain it to her. I'd never been able to explain it. Martha could adopt any persona. People thought that she was delightful. But life with her was nearly impossible. No degree of good fortune could satisfy her. She could love you and hate you at the same time. Occasionally, the facade would crack and a victim—

typically a waiter or porter—would see what I saw: a mood swing or an eruption of anger over some minor infraction. Otherwise, it was my hell alone to bear. I eventually drove her away, taking every advantage to fan the flames of marital discord in my haste. I traded the wrath of Martha for the cold mistrust of family and friends. They sided with her.

Sweaty volunteers labored over the steaming pots and the pungent mixed smoke of seaweed and firewood. The waiters' bustle grew more intense. My mother's old friend continued her diatribe, punctuated with a barb about how I might want to "help out" at the club sometime. Before I could describe my afternoon working in the sandy ditch, a young woman called out from atop a folding chair: "Everyone, please take your seats."

I detoured past the banquet table to ladle another serving of punch. I wedged and apologized my way through the closely spaced tables to find Elizabeth. I placed my hands on Foster's shoulders as I passed behind him.

"Nice new grey boat you have there," I said.

"Huh?"

I squeezed into my folding chair, adjacent to the band. I said hello to Elizabeth again. "You know Maura Garren, don't you?" she asked. I turned and found myself dinner mates with the lead bridge hen. One of my hands held rum punch. She took the other, apathetically.

"We've met," she said, looking at me. "I'm friends with your wife."

Mrs. Steeves' niece, Allison, squeezed in behind me. She put her arms around my neck. I turned to see who it was.

"Hi, sweetie. Are you going to dance with me later?" Allison asked.

"Uh, sure."

"Great." She raised her eyebrows briefly as if to share an unspoken secret, and then disappeared as quickly as she had come.

Maura Garren glared at me. "You're not—you wouldn't—you haven't done anything untoward with that child, have you? You know she has—psychological issues."

"Of course not. I don't even know her."

I couldn't have been more uncomfortable.

"It will be a few minutes before dinner is served," I volunteered to whomever would listen. "I think this would be a good time to check on the boys."

I sidled my way out and walked up the hill to the house. The sun was going down. "Boys?" I yelled from the front lawn. Nobody answered. There was a disturbance from the trashcans. I dashed out the back door, through the roses, to the shed. I pulled the lids from the cans. *Aha!* I ran next door to Janet's parents' house with my find: a bag of unfamiliar trash.

I banged on the door. Janet's father, Frank, opened slowly.

"Frank, where's Janet?"

"Out somewhere."

"Then what's this?" I held up the garbage like a bloody head.

"It looks like garbage."

"It *is* garbage."

Frank hung on the door, waiting for an explanation. I considered how it would sound—me recounting my argument with his daughter, culminating with an accusation of her using our garbage cans for Frank's family's garbage. Frank waited. I decided I'd be better off changing the subject, though I maintained my belief in Janet's guilt.

There were some construction papers on the table behind Frank. I dropped the garbage and prodded him about his house renovations. He took the bait, invited me in, slid his glasses down his nose, poured two scotches and unrolled a drawing. I downed the whiskey, thinking that would excuse me from a long tour of the plans. He reflexively poured a second scotch and mulled over the drawings. I asked a few polite questions and received onerously thorough answers. I could hear the band warming up at the club.

"Frank, I gotta get back to the clambake," I petitioned at last.

"Finish your drink."

I threw back the whiskey and jogged down to the club. The lights were low under the tent. The band played. Elizabeth danced with Roger. The waitress poured tepid coffee. I prospected for silverware.

Mine was the only uncleared plate. A one-clawed lobster sat in a cold puddle.

"I gave Lilly your sole," Maura Garren shouted to me, unapologetically. "The girls took your clams."

I leaned back in the folding chair. The loudness of the band made Maura Garren my only practical dinner mate. I tried to answer her barbs with nods. When she honked out something more complicated, a question about parenting without Martha, I had to shout to be heard. My breath respired from the bottom of Frank's twelve-year-old scotch bottle. Maura Garren grimaced and waved me off. She refused an offer to dance. I picked at the cold lobster to the strains of the band.

Damn it, I said to myself. *She thinks I'm a drunk.*

I excused myself to no one a second time and left the table to check on the boys. They were home, as they should have been. I was saying my goodnights when I heard another disturbance at the garbage cans. I dashed out in mid-sentence, rounded the shed and tripped over a skunk. It regained its footing, turned, aimed and sprayed a direct hit. I stumbled, gagging, back to the house. Banging on the door, I summoned the boys to come outside.

"Dad, there's someone at the back door," I heard the younger one call from beyond the upstairs window.

"It's me, damn it," I yelled. "Get out here!"

The boys slunk out timidly, keeping an eye out for a skunk.

"Is that *you*?" the older boy asked.

"Yes," I said, spitting to get rid of the taste. "One of you get some vinegar or tomato juice from the cabinet."

The younger boy disappeared. A wave of the odor struck me anew. I gagged, choked and threw up. The older boy backed away from me as if I were in the process of exploding. Bent at the waist and motioning toward the beach, I commissioned him: "Go down to the club and explain to the people at Elizabeth's table what happened."

I learned later that he couldn't tell which was Elizabeth's table. She wasn't there. She was strolling the moonlit beach with Roger.

Resourcefully, the boy relayed the message to the bandleader, who announced that I wouldn't be returning because I'd gotten skunked and thrown up.

Sunday, June 30th

The boys slept late in the mounting summer heat. Eventually, they'd sweat themselves awake. I sat red-eyed in the kitchen, enjoying a last sip of coffee before the communion fast on liquids, thinking that Jesus might make an exception for coffee if he tried it. When I pushed back from the table, I felt something pinch at my heel. An ant— I looked at the floor. Jesus, loaves and fishes: Ants everywhere! I jumped from the chair and stomped at them with my sole. The survivors scattered and set panic to the swarm. I swept them from the cracks. They emerged anew, like blood from an unstemmed wound. It was miraculous. But after ten minutes, I left the ants in God's hands. I had to get to church.

I stepped into the summer chapel fifteen minutes early—the victim of a Mass schedule change sometime in the years since I'd last attended. I chose a seat halfway back, near an open window, feeling penitent and alone in the hard pew. I'd forgotten how hot the chapel could be.

Slowly at first, and then more quickly, Catholics came marching in. More than once, children slid into seats fore and aft of me and were subsequently tugged from the pew in favor of another spot by a whispering parent. As seating became tighter, a well-defined, vacant semi-circle formed around me. By the opening procession, it looked as if something had taken a bite out of the congregation and left me at the radial center. Embarrassed that I might smell, but more deeply concerned that my reputation might be at issue, I glanced around for an escape. Then, I reasoned that I should stay long enough to get credit for attending. We stood, sat, kneeled and muttered as a family. The Latin liturgy eventually quieted to a low mumble, signaling the sermon. I leaned back for Father Ivan's homily.

"Peter tells us that we must do good works. We must be contributing members of the faith. Desire isn't enough. As the old saying goes, 'The road to hell is paved with good intentions.'"

Father Ivan paused to glare at the parishioners standing in the back of the hot chapel, where they'd escaped to enjoy a breath of air. "There are open seats up here," he offered. Nobody moved. He continued with his sermon: "And we all know that bad intentions will get you there just as well."

The congregation chuckled politely.

"Most of us were baptized before we were of an age to consent to Christianity. Our parents' intentions were that we be followers in the footsteps of Jesus—the footsteps that led to the cross. Their hope was that we would be generous members of the church. Fail their good intentions and we fail God.

"We might pray that our fellow man—Christian and heathen— will do good. But we cannot alter his intentions or actions through prayer. This is because God gives us free will. All of us. He lets us choose our paths, right or wrong. How then may we ask Him to guide the paths of others? Why should we ask that Johnny study more, or our young daughters stay away from boys? God will not intervene on our behalves. God will not intervene on behalf of your children either, as this would violate the free will of others. Rather, we must help our fellow human beings see His good intentions, and to do *our* bidding, in His name. God will *not* change the heart of another or decide their fate on your behalf. Just as He will not change your path at the bidding of another. If we wish for improvement, then we must make it happen ourselves, and as a community. We must have good intentions, and act on them.

"God showed His resolve for free will when He gave up His Son to die on the cross. He gave His son grace. And He will be there for you too. When you have been struck down, He will send you an angel. When you are overwhelmed in a sea of despair, He will send you an angel. When your world is on fire, He will send you an angel. He will not help you in earthly ways. But, God will be there to meet you once you have suffered the last stone.

"As the old saying goes: 'God helps those who help themselves.' Help God by opening your hearts and wallets and make a contrite donation to this ministry. Amen."

There was coughing, money collection, Latin and tinkling bells.

Parishioners filed into communion lines. I waited until most of the other communicants had received before taking my turn. Father Ivan had already returned to the altar. The remaining hosts were administered by a deacon, dressed in a black cassock with a white surplice. I wasn't certain whether he registered the odor of the skunk or whether the ceremony had changed over the years but, in lieu of "Body of Christ," he said "Jesus Christ!" when I stepped up. I returned to my pew. The coughing and fidgeting grew in volume. There was more Latin and some housekeeping. Then, the words the congregation longed for: "The Mass is ended, go in peace."

"Thank God," I said.

"A few parting notes," bellowed Father Ivan over the ebbing tide of parishioners. "We will be getting together after Mass to finish organizing the church picnic, which is coming up on the Fourth. If you cannot attend, but wish to help, please see Mrs. Steeves, Mrs. Peterson or Mr. Smith. Don't forget to bring something. The details are in the bulletin."

No! Leave me out of it, I thought. *I don't like priests. I don't like picnics—and I don't like ants.*

Ten minutes later, Mrs. Peterson, Father Ivan and I met in the rectory adjacent to the main stone church, in town. Mrs. Steeves wasn't present. I smelled like a skunk; the two of them told me so without reservation. I was at one end of a long banquet table. They were together at the other. It felt like a legal proceeding. The little breeze we shared passed out through an open door behind me. Father Ivan got directly to business, speaking to me as though I had a notion of what had been planned so far.

"The parishioners are bringing salads and hors d'oeuvres. The church will supply hotdogs and hamburgers. What are the bridge ladies providing? Snacks and desserts?"

"Just desserts," Mrs. Peterson responded.

"Well, be sure to get the word out as soon as possible," he said to both of us. "Time is running short. We still need people to cook and clean up."

Father Ivan asked Loretta Peterson to help organize activities and games. "You'll need plenty of volunteers," he said.

"Oh, that's all set. Though, we could use more young men to help with the games," said Mrs. Peterson, looking at me with a raised brow. I stared back but offered no response. "Jack, do you suppose you can get some young men to help with the games?"

"I like your hat," I said.

"We're starting at eleven-thirty and going until six," Father Ivan continued. "The fireworks are on the bay that evening, so we'll want to be all cleaned up and out of there by sunset."

I was beside myself; the Fourth of July regatta would be taking place the same afternoon. I would have to miss it for a crappy church picnic. I wondered why one would even want a church picnic on the Fourth when there were so many other activities planned.

Janet approached as I crossed the road to the house in the late morning sun, sweating in my church clothes. "It smelled so bad here that none of us slept last night," she said. "I just want you to know that."

"So stop putting trash in my trash," I barked back.

"Are you an idiot? It's not us; we have our own cans. But we can't even leave the house at night without tripping over one of your raccoons or skunks."

"My raccoons? I swear, Janet, if I catch you near those cans I am going to knock you into them."

"Listen, you jerk. It's not us."

I turned to go back into the house, muttering "Fatty" just loud enough to be heard.

The boys were at the kitchen table, sitting among the ants, eating cookies.

"Dad, we've got ants."

"Ach," I said as I passed through, waving a hand behind me.

The younger boy went back to talking to his brother as I departed the room. "Black ants are the color of death, but red ants are the color of love."

Upstairs, I peeled the church clothes off into a soggy pile. I pulled on shorts, a light shirt and transferred the belongings from my pockets. The open air on my sweaty arms and legs felt wonderful. I skipped barefoot out of the house with the delight of a child released to the playground. I slowed at the end of the driveway and looked down the hill toward the beach. It was going to be a beautiful beach day. I decided to take the boys crabbing. I found them upstairs, reading comics.

"Who wants to go crabbing?"

"Nah," they said in unison.

"Why not?"

"Crabbing is boring," said the older one.

"No, it's not. C'mon!" This didn't stir them. "I'm going with or without you."

I went into the shed to get a bucket and a piece of string.

"C'mon, boys," I called out.

I walked down the hill alone. Upon reaching the shore, I looked to see if my boat was at its mooring yet. All the others rocked gently at theirs. Foster's "battleship," apparently not attended to since it arrived, sat low in the water, swamped.

The tide was halfway out. I waded into the water to find a mussel. I smashed one with a rock and tied it to a string. Finding a flat rock to sit upon, I dipped the mussel into the water. Crabs came from all directions. One-by-one and two-by-two I hoisted them over the wall of the bucket and shook them from the mussel until I'd captured dozens. I looked around for someone to celebrate my good fortune.

Two little girls walked along the beach in my direction.

"Hey, hey!" I called out. "Come see this. Come see the crabs."

The two stopped briefly and then hastened up toward the road, cutting a wider path around me.

"Hey, wait!" I shouted.

I stood up with the crab bucket and started walking toward them. They hustled a little farther away, eventually breaking into a jog. I gave up, returned to the water's edge. With nobody to care, I spilled the crabs back into the bay. Looking back out at the moorings I said, "Damn it. Where's my damn boat? We're supposed to race today."

I left the crab bucket wedged in the rocks and walked off the beach into the street. I went up the road toward the post office, thinking I'd place a scathing phone call to the boatyard. The phone was in a locked portion of the post office, this being Sunday. The next public phone was half a mile away, in town. I stood on the step, biting my lip and pondering my options. There'd be no point driving to the boatyard; they'd be largely closed today as well.

Staring at the locked door, I let myself become engrossed in the notices. They were predominantly FBI wanted posters. The offenses included criminal assault, embezzlement, mail fraud, theft, child molestation, arson, statutory rape, attempted murder. Most of the subjects were men. Some were women. I studied the faces, looking for neighbors and people from town. I thought about posting my own FBI wanted ad with a likeness of Martha and a warning that said: "Dangerous! Shoot on sight." Or perhaps one of Janet that simply said, "Fat."

On the other side of the doorway was a poster that challenged the homeowners in the beach area to decorate their homes for the Fourth of July. To the winner, a pie baked by Mrs. Steeves. The Fourth was Thursday. The boys and I could dress the old house in bunting and red, white and blue streamers, I mused. That same thought tugged me back to the question of the whereabouts of my red, white and blue boat.

"I want my damn boat!" I bellowed to the hot, empty street from atop the post office steps.

I walked back to the Crescent Club and took up a spot on the porch—feet on the railing. Before long, the porch filled in around me. I said hello to a dozen passers-by, carting sail bags and coolers. Martin Hoover, a childhood acquaintance, dropped his load to stop and chat. His ten-year-old son, Timmy, was with him. I stood up to greet them.

"Hey, Smith," said Martin. "I heard you had a run-in with the bridge club the other day."

"I smell a skunk," the boy said, looking around.

"That was—well, someone had a drink with me and snuck out as the bridge league came in—Phony McPipe."

"What's that? McPipe? Some sort of mixed drink?" asked Martin.

"Dad, I think there's a skunk nearby," whined Timmy.

"No, no. Not McPipe. What's his name? "I stumbled through a mental block trying to recall McPipe's real name. Finally it came to me. "Bob Malinowski!" I barked.

"How do you do?" I heard from behind me. I turned around to find Phony McPipe Malinowski holding a cup of coffee in one hand. The other chalky hand stretched out for any takers.

"Hey, Cap'n Bob. How are you? How was your winter?" Martin sang out as he edged past me to shake McPipe's claw.

"Something really smells funny," Timmy said.

"Fine," said McPipe. "How's the family?"

"You remember my son, Timmy."

"How do you do, Timmy?" asked McPipe.

Timmy screwed up his face further.

"Thanks for taking us on as race committee today," said Martin.

"My pleasure," said McPipe. Then to me, "Hello again, Jack." Then to all of us: "And now if you'll excuse me, I've got to ready the race committee boat."

I watched McPipe enter the clubhouse, go into the men's lavatory and never reappear.

Martin turned back to me: "So, you were saying something about pipes?"

"Jack?" I heard from behind me. It was Elizabeth; I was saved.

Martin and Liz said their hellos and Martin excused himself and his son.

"Do you want to race today? I've got my brother's boat, and I need a skipper," Liz said.

"Where's Roger?" I asked.

"Roger?" she asked as if the question seemed foreign, "I don't know."

"I mean, aren't you going with him?" I asked.

"No. I don't even know where he is," she said.

"Foster, then?"

"Foster? I don't think he even likes to sail," she said. "He's a golfer."

"Why did he buy a boat then?"

"He did?"

"Yes, that one," I said, pointing to the battleship.

"I don't think that's his," she said. "At least, he didn't mention it. I heard that Father Ivan bought a boat. Maybe that's Father Ivan's?"

She wrinkled her nose. "Jack, is that a new cologne?"

Elizabeth and I had a quick lunch and then rode the club launch boat out to her brother's sailboat. The afternoon had grown hot and the breeze was very light. There were a number of other crews getting ready to sail. We spilled our sail bag into the cockpit and sorted through the sails, choosing who would rig what.

The time between August, when a boat is stored for the winter, and June, when she is re-commissioned, is long enough to forget specifics about one's own rigging, especially if the boat is new to them. Looking over the equipment on Liz's brother's boat, I compared what I saw to recollections of my own boat.

"I don't think that cleat is in that same spot on my boat. Or is it?"

"What's that?" asked Elizabeth. Her voice was muffled. She was busy in the cockpit. On her hands and knees, her head and shoulders extended underneath the deck.

"I recognize that cleat," I repeated loudly, "but I don't remember seeing it placed there."

Forgetting how confined she was in the space beneath the deck, she turned to give her attention to me. Then, *BANG!* She hit her head.

"Ow! Jesus," she wailed.

I rushed to her aid. She backed out on her knees. There was a little bleeding centered upon a swelling lump on her forehead, where she'd hit a metal bolt. Her hand went to the lump.

"Is it bad?" she asked looking at the blood on her palm.

"No, you're fine." It kept bleeding. I handed her a church bulletin from my pocket to blot the wound.

"What was it you were trying to say to me?"

"Only that I don't remember the layout of my boat being like this. But thinking about it, I can't remember my layout exactly."

"Oh—," she said, plainly annoyed that my musings had caused the accident. After a few minutes, she lost her preoccupation with the welted egg on her forehead and we resumed rigging. We dropped off the mooring and joined a parade of Zips inching toward the race committee boat and the starting line.

The first starts of the season brought some confusion. Some skippers had forgotten the rights of way under sail. Others never knew them. There was a gentle collision between two boats at the start, followed by some yelling and the posting of a red protest flag. Later, these two skippers would make their grievances before a protest committee, chaired by Phony McPipe.

Elizabeth and I made a good start in the dying breeze. We crept around the windward mark in third place. But at just about the moment that half of the boats had come around, the wind died altogether. The fleet rocked and swayed sleepily, making little progress. Whenever the wind dies, you can talk to the people in neighboring boats, and speaking a little louder to the boats beyond them, and with a shout or a wave to the boats beyond them. The relationships in life's journey become becalmed before you: old sweethearts, parents' friends, friends' children.

Elizabeth stared at the horizon.

"How come you never asked me to marry you?" she said.

"What?"

"Just kidding—maybe. But, we make a good couple."

Elizabeth and I were close friends growing up. We had a few flings, but we were never a couple. Elizabeth eventually married the wrong person and stayed married for a long time. The situation hadn't been right for children, but I knew she wished she had had some. With only a few childbearing years left, there was no man in the picture.

"Well, you never know what might happen," I said, thinking about sex.

In the heat and the still air the flies found us, providing me a welcome respite from relationship talk. Eventually, the race committee called off the race and Liz and I accepted a tow back to the mooring.

"Would you like to come over for dinner?" I asked.

"Okay," she said, her face lumpy and red.

"Come at six."

I had scarcely seen the boys in the last few days, but I was relieved when they said that they were staying at a friend's house for the evening. I wanted the place to myself and Liz. With just a half hour to prepare for dinner, the challenge now was finding something to make. I took stock of the groceries at hand. I had potatoes, asparagus, eggs, tuna, canned peas, butter, bread, flour, cornstarch and spices. *What could I do with that? Something with eggs and potatoes, maybe.* I started boiling water. I threw in a handful of bullion cubes, potatoes and peas. Stew! At 5:45, there was a knock on the door.

She's early. I was concerned that dinner wasn't close to being ready—that I wasn't even sure what I was making. Still, I was glad to have Liz there. But, there was no shadow on the screen door at this time of day. I could plainly see it was Chloe.

"Hi," she said.

I looked past her for the spawn. "Where's your boy?"

"Mom is looking after him tonight," she said. "I brought you dinner."

Chloe beamed and reached beyond the purview of the door and

retrieved a hidden stew pot and a paper bag.

"Ta-da!" she sang.

I started to explain that I was expecting company.

Chloe shouldered her way through the door and dropped the pot on the table, crushing an ant.

"Hot!" she said.

"How can that be so hot?" I asked, again looking beyond her and out through the door for clues. All I could see was her bicycle.

"I have a hurricane stove in the basket. Wind-proof. That reminds me. I always forget to blow that out."

She turned to go back outside. I took her arm.

"Chloe?" I hesitated. "I have company coming for dinner tonight—I can't ask you to stay."

"Oh—" she said. "Okay, well, it's no big deal. I'll go down to the club with it. Can I use your bathroom?"

"Sure," I said.

She disappeared around the corner.

I stood in the kitchen next to the stew and the mystery bag. I listened for any sign of Chloe's return. None apparent, I quietly opened the lid. The smell was wonderful: a bourguinon with mushrooms and huge chunks of beef. The bag was stuffed with warm rolls.

"Can I have a taste?" I shouted through the bathroom door.

"Sure," came the muffled answer.

What possessed me next, I cannot defend: I ladled part of the pot into a saucepan and stole three of the rolls. I hid the purloined stew under the sink. Then, horrified to see that the pot was now more than half empty, I hastily replenished the void with my own stew. An uninvited giant raw potato splashed in, soaking the table and me.

I heard the toilet flush beyond the closed door. With no time left, I dropped the lid and took a swipe at the table with a dishtowel, then threw it and the ladle clattering behind me as Chloe rounded the corner.

"Well, sorry that didn't work out," she said, collecting the bag and the pot.

I followed her out to the bicycle, feeling guilty, but looking forward to the taste of stolen food. She positioned the pot into the Sterno stove and pushed the bag in beside it. She walked the bicycle carefully out to the street, mounted it and started down the hill.

The wind fanned the edge of the bag, licked by the Sterno flame. By the time Chloe reached the bottom of the hill, the bag was fully aflame. She noticed all at once, swerved off the road and crashed the bicycle near the swamp. I hid behind a tree. She slid from under the bike, stood up, brushed herself off and limped in a circle. By now, the flames had consumed the bag and it had smoldered out. She stared quizzically at the inexplicable giant white potato that had rolled out onto the grass. Then she looked back up the hill toward the house and me. At last, she picked up the spilled bicycle and limped toward the club.

I was back in the house for just a moment before there came another knock at the kitchen door. *Ah*, I said to myself, thinking Liz had arrived. But again, the screen did nothing to keep the largest bugs out; it was Lilly. She had been watering my garden as I had facetiously suggested.

"You know, there used to be a septic tank over there and I think it may be falling in," she started.

"Lilly, I've got company arriving soon," I said.

"Well it used to be there," she said, pointing out into the yard. "And I think it's—"

I cut her off. "That's fascinating Lilly, but I have company—."

"Well you should really have a—"

"Fine. Thank you, Lilly." I pushed the inner door shut for the first time in a week. Lilly looked dully through the shut door window glass, then turned gingerly and waddled back toward the garden.

A while later, came another knock at the door. I opened it, hoping again that it would be Liz. This time it was Mrs. Steeves' niece, Allison. She rushed through the open door, jumped up on her tiptoes and kissed my cheek. After my talking-to from the lead bridge hen, Maura Garren, I was now very aware of the trouble Allison presented. This girl was precocious because she had "psychological issues."

"I was thinking, what would it be like if we were married?" she asked.

"What? How old are you?"

"Eighteen. Do you want to see my boobs?"

Before I could answer, she pulled her shirt up to her neck. They were beautiful.

"Stop that," I insisted.

She smiled and shook her whole torso left and right so they shimmied.

"Put those away. You have to go now," I said.

Just then, there was a knock on the other door. Allison pouted and pulled her shirt down.

"I want to show you everything," she whispered.

"No—. Well, maybe. Wait. How old are you, really?"

"Jack?" A voice called through the opposite doorway. It was Elizabeth, finally.

"You have to go," I hissed to Allison. She kissed me again and started out the door she'd come in, but not before Elizabeth helped herself to the handle on the opposite door. I turned to see her enter. Suddenly, Elizabeth looked thick and old.

"Who was that?" she asked, craning her head to follow the form making its way out through the trellis.

"A neighbor. Nobody."

"Well, sorry I'm late. I was at the club tending to Chloe. She was pretty scraped up and upset. She had an accident on her bicycle coming down the hill from your house. You could have asked her to stay. As it was, she lost a whole pot of stew when her bike fell over. And she looked even more upset when I told her I was coming here for dinner."

"Oh no. That's awful," I said. "She arrived unannounced; I was expecting *you*. I mean, I could have asked her to stay."

"Well, she'll be alright. So, what have you got for me? I'm starving."

"Stew," I declared.

The lump on Elizabeth's forehead from the sailing accident that afternoon had become bruised and swollen. She raised a hand to feel it. "Stew?" she repeated, leaving room for questions, but not asking them.

We had a couple of gin and tonics. I brushed the ants from the rolls and the saucepan and heated the food. The asparagus gave me a plausible escape from any suspicion that Liz might have had regarding the stew; Chloe certainly hadn't mentioned asparagus.

Our dinner by candlelight was pleasant enough. A few after-dinner drinks loosened the mood. Liz and I were in the kitchen cleaning up the plates. I'd grabbed her ass a couple of times already and I was making moves for the living room at dusk when I heard the distinct sound of a garbage can.

"Hang on," I said, and ran out the kitchen door toward the shed. In the blackness, I could see movement—not an animal, a person— the height of a person. I ran full force and lunged at the figure, taking a few cans down at the same time. We tumbled together into the space where the exterior wall of the shed meets the bare earth, wedged together into the corner, me on top.

I had wholly expected my fall to be padded by ample Janet. Instead, a slight figure beneath me shifted and groaned. "My shoulder," it said. A porch light came on across the way. In an instant, vindication turned to horror as I realized I was atop Mrs. Steeves. I dismounted and tended to her on my knees. She was soiled in the scant light. A bread wrapper stuck to her cheek. "Mrs. Steeves, I'm so sorry! You're alright, right?" I pleaded.

"My shoulder," she moaned.

Liz, now rounding the corner of the shed, rushed to her side.

"Agnes?" she asked. "What happened? Are you okay?"

Liz cradled Mrs. Steeves and walked her back home. She turned to flash me an accusatory glance as she reached Mrs. Steeves' house across the way.

Constable Howard deposed me in the kitchen.

"Were you drinkin'?" he demanded.

"Well, I mean, yeah. We had a few drinks."

I could see the fire department ambulance pulling away across the street. Fortunately, Mrs. Steeves wasn't in it. A crowd of neighbors and gawkers from the Crescent Club stood at the edge of my lawn, waiting to see what the constable would do.

"You like tackling old ladies, do ya?"

"Of course not, but I thought—"

"I ought to arrest you. Or knock your head in."

"Well, honestly officer—," I said, getting up. Constable Howard gave me a solid backward shove. The chair groaned as it retreated across the kitchen floor with me in it, nearly toppling. Janet's spying form swayed through the screen door, off in the shadows.

"You've got a reputation," Constable Howard said. "And I don't like you. You can't seem to stay out of trouble."

Constable Howard left. I went over to Mrs. Steeves' to see if I could make good. She lay on the couch with an ice pack. Chloe limped from the kitchen with a fresh replacement. Standing out of sight of the others, Allison blew me a kiss. Liz met me at the door. Her welt was raised and angry.

"Why was she putting trash into my cans?" I asked.

"So she wouldn't have to haul her own full cans to the curb with her bad shoulder. Martha told her it would be okay."

Monday, July 1st

I was the most unpopular person in town.

I woke to a glorious morning, full of promise. I opened my bedroom porch doors a little wider to catch the breeze. Squinting against the glare of the sparkling bay, I could see a disturbance at the ferry dock. A woman slapped something out of the grip of a deckhand, and then pointed to the ground where it lay as if to suggest he should pick it up again. *Rude*, I thought. Then, she turned and pointed up the hill toward the house. I'd seen that conformation many times; someone was being told what to do. *It can't be.* But it was.

It was Martha.

{ MARTHA SMITH }

A Few Days Earlier

I wanted my life back—my husband and my children. But more
urgently, I needed money. I was a little hungover, too. I sat in
the banker's waiting room with felt wallpaper, vinyl chairs and a
tulip lamp, listening to the typewriters and eavesdropping on the
receptionist. She was clearly on the phone with a friend, making
me wait unnecessarily. I walked up to the desk and knocked on its
surface, politely.

"Excuse me. I've been here for twenty minutes."

She covered the mouthpiece and said, "If you'll just have a seat,
I'll check on Mr. Burke."

I leaned in, looked her in the eye and swept her stack of
paperwork to the floor with my forearm. "Tell him I want to see him
now. I have other things to do, princess."

She glared, pursed her lips to call me a bitch, and then backed down, saying into the phone: "Gotta go." She buzzed Burke's intercom. "Smith is short on time."

"Send her in," crackled his response.

As I entered Burke's office, another banker slid out the door behind me and shut it. I studied the desk. It seemed that every document had Jack's and my name on it. I looked Mr. Burke in the eye and gathered that he and the other fellow had been delaying me on purpose.

"You made me wait," I said.

"Please sit down," he said, nervously.

"I'm not interested in sitting. Just give me the money."

"Well, I can't—," he said. "There's a problem and I can't really— not without Jack's signature. I realize that these are your assets too, but they are jointly owned, and until the divorce is finalized, I have to protect both of your interests. But if Jack is willing to give me a call, I suppose—"

"Well, he can't. There are no phones on the island. Why can't you just give me half? It's half mine. How much is there?"

"I don't know that, Mrs. Smith. Not until the courts have decided. Is there postal delivery?"

"How much is there? I have a right to know."

"It's difficult to say. There's some real estate—the beach house— How can I reach Jack?"

"Listen buster, it's my money too."

"By law, I have to have Jack's agreement. Will he be back in the area anytime soon?"

"Oh, just send him a damn letter," I said. I turned to leave and then turned back. "What will you send to him?"

"Well, a note explaining that you are looking for an advance on the settlement. If he agrees to give you some money, then I can go ahead with your request. If not, then you will have to take it up with him or the courts. I simply manage the funds."

"When? When will you send it?"

"What?" Burke asked.

"The fucking letter!"

Burke stumbled over a response. "Well, I suppose—as soon as we can. I'll need a response, of course," he said.

"Don't send it until I tell you to," I instructed. "I want to call Jack first."

"Okay—" he said, pausing. "But I thought you said there were no phones."

"Are you accusing me of lying? Because if you are, I'll have this place crawling with lawyers in ten minutes. As it is, I think you're hiding something."

"I assure you Mrs. Smith— Do you want to call me—tell me when it's okay to send the note to Jack; the letter; your proposal?"

"Yes," I said, "I'll call you. Have the letter ready, and have it say that he has to give me half."

"I can't do that, Mrs. Smith. But I will write him concerning our conversation."

"Listen, you work for me too. Half the money in this bank is mine. So don't fuck with me."

I slid one of Burke's business cards into my bra. The staff stood in a hushed semi-circle in the waiting room, watching me go. "Nice decor. Chumps," I hissed. I stepped out onto the hot city street and ducked into the shadows of a bar across the way for a bite to eat and a single-malt to calm the nerves.

I couldn't possibly have survived on what Jack had given me. I decided that I would have the banker send the letter to Jack. Then I'd intercept it, craft a response and authorize the money myself. After all, the money was mine. I shouldn't have had to ask permission to get it—especially from him, after what he did to me and the boys: the fighting, the separation, his gold-digging whores, the court orders.

It was all wrong. Jack charmed his way through life, and he always got what he wanted. He was popular, smart, successful in business, funny and handsome. But, when he became too successful, he forgot the ones who had helped him get there, including me. He stayed out late. He went on business trips with his female employees. He'd come home and accuse me of all kinds of crazy behavior. Then he ditched me. I simply wanted to be his wife. I still loved him. Everything would have been fine if Jack had simply talked to me.

Back at the house, I gave the living room a once-over with the dust rag, stopping to marvel at the pictures of Mark and John, now twelve and fourteen. I closed my eyes and imagined the smell of their hair. *I am their mother.*

There was a knock. I cracked the front door, letting in some of the summer evening heat. Dick stood on the front step.

"Let me in! The ice cream's melting," he said. I swung the door open and gave him a hug through the outstretched sundaes. He kissed me. It wasn't long before we were both naked in the living room.

"Nice suitcase. Where are you going?" he asked, spying the luggage in the front hall.

"Nowhere. Those are winter clothes," I told him. "Do you want a scotch?"

"No."

"Well, if you don't mind, I will," I said on my way to the pantry.

He spent the night. I crept out at dawn, leaving Dick in a tangle of covers. I rolled the car silently down the driveway and headed for the ferry docks of New London. There was no room for the car on the first ferry, so I left it behind. I threw up twice on the way over. When we reached the island, the other passengers left me behind, sick. I had to hire one of the teenage dockhands. He took my bags down and then signaled a friend to drive me up the hill. The boy was cute. While I was waiting for the car to come around, I asked him about the return schedule. He looked toward his clipboard. A horsefly buzzed around him in the hot morning sun. He shooed it away repeatedly. Eventually, it landed on the clipboard and I took a swat at it, accidentally knocking the clipboard from the boy's hand.

"There he is. I got him," I said, pointing to the mashed horsefly on the ground.

"Thanks," he said, bending down to retrieve the board. I stepped closer.

"I'm Martha." I said to him.

He stood back up, face in mine.

"Oh. Nice to meet you. I'm Rob. That's Evan," he said. He backed away and pointed at the car pulling into the parking area.

"Nice to meet you too," I said. I rummaged through my bag for tip money. I found an airplane-sized bottle of rum and gave that to him instead. I pointed toward the house. "Can I get a ride up the hill?"

"Well, that's Evan," he repeated again, like it would mean something to me.

"*That's Evan?* Can you say anything else?" I asked.

"I mean, he can give you a ride, maybe," Rob said, starting to look uncomfortable.

"Does he like rum too?" I asked.

"Uhh—" was all Rob could muster.

I walked over to Evan's car and made a quick arrangement. I watched to be sure he loaded the bags into the trunk and then I slid in the passenger's side.

"Where to?" Evan asked.

"Just up the hill— the green house with red trim."

"The Smith house?" he asked.

"Yes, please."

"Oh," he said, glancing over. "Are you Katrin?"

"I'm Martha Smith—Jack's wife. Do I look like some German whore?"

Evan shrunk into the driver's side door, unsure of the mistake he had made. Katrin was the reason Jack left me and ruined the boys' lives. A West German girl under Jack's employ—she lured him away with her twenty-something-year-old body. I swore that if I found that gold-digging, Nazi bitch here on the island I would beat her senseless. At the top of the hill, Evan spilled the bags carelessly out onto the driveway and sped off like a coward.

"Asshole!" I screamed after him.

Angry and hot, I stood at the edge of the driveway and scanned the house. There was a fat woman leaning on a windowsill, cupping her eyes to see inside. She seemed big for Jack's taste.

"You fat-assed, Nazi, gold-digging whore!" I screamed. "Get away from my house and stay away from my husband."

I threw my cosmetics bag at her. It missed and exploded on house's shakes beside her. She stood frozen for a moment. I followed with a lipstick that had fallen out of the bag. It spiraled end-over-end, clipping her on the shoulder. Her fat frame knocked down part of the barnyard fence as she chugged away toward the safety of the house next door. A screen door slammed behind her.

I stood for a moment, wondering to myself why the German woman would run into a neighbor's house. At length, I decided that I might have picked on the wrong person, though whoever she was, she deserved to be chased away—Peeping Tom.

I turned to collect my bags, as it was apparent that nobody was coming out to help me. The house was a mess. There were dishes in the sink. Clothes were draped over chairs. Toys blocked my way. There was no sign of Mark or John. I scanned the living room. There were two framed seascapes I'd never seen before. I felt my bile rise. There were new pillow cushions. I kicked one across the living room. Every unexplained doily made me madder. I pulled a print off the wall in disgust, dragged my bags upstairs to the master bedroom, and then returned to the dining room. I searched the cabinets for some relief, finding at last a bottle of scotch. It tasted like dust.

"Yuck, this is awful," I said. Then, as punctuation, "Fucking Germans."

The kitchen door slammed. I jumped up, spun around the corner—ready to spar with anyone. But it was my two boys. My heart melted.

"My babies," I sang out, arms extended.

"Mom!" They ran over for a group hug. "We missed you."

If there was ever a moment of vindication, this was it. The judge had been out of his mind when he made the custody arrangements. My boys needed me. Forever.

"Oh, you poor things. You're so tanned and thin. Have you been living outdoors? Has your father been feeding you?"

"Yes," John said, "Dad's been good to us."

"Where is he?" I demanded.

"We don't know," the boys agreed hesitantly. "We haven't seen him today."

"Oh, no. You poor things. Did you get breakfast?"

"No. I mean, yes," said Mark. "We had breakfast at Nicky's."

"You have to go to the neighbors' to eat?"

"No, Mom. You don't understand. We spent the night there. We spend a lot of nights there."

"That's horrible! *Where is your father?*"

There were footsteps on the porch. I ran into the front room, expecting to see Jack through the windows. Instead, there was a stringy-haired woman with a bedraggled child in tow. A bicycle leaned up against the tree.

"So *that's* Katrin," I hissed through an inhale. "*They have a child?*"

I flung the porch door so hard that it slammed open.

"What the hell is this, Little Hitler? Sprechen Sie Deutsch, klein Kraut?" I demanded of the boy.

He screamed and his pants fell down. The stringy-haired woman recoiled in horror, dropped a loaf of bread, pulled the child sideways off the porch, and dragged him and the bicycle off the property. She picked the bare-assed wunderkind up in one arm and ran the bicycle down the hill, as if fleeing a fire.

"Mom, Mom!" The boys ran up behind me to intervene. "Please don't yell. Please don't yell."

I collected myself, sat on a porch chair with a fresh scotch and apologized calmly to them. Believing the stringy-haired woman to have been the German, I said to the boys: "I'm sorry. I just hate that woman."

"We don't like her either," said John.

"She's seen us naked," said Mark.

"What?" My anger ignited anew. "I don't want Jack's whore anywhere near my boys."

I sent the boys out to find and retrieve their father. I took another swig of the cheap scotch and then marched over to get the latest news from Mrs. Steeves. But there was no discussion of the German woman; there was no place for it. What Mrs. Steeves told me— Jack had assaulted her the night before. And he was drunk!

"Well, it wasn't exactly like that," Agnes Steeves said. "I think that Jack thought I was a burglar or something. I must say that my shoulder is feeling better this morning. And I think it's good to have someone watching over the neighborhood, don't you?"

"But Agnes, my husband treated you very roughly!"

"It's okay—," she said trailing off.

I felt that Agnes must be a forgiving soul—like me. And like me, Jack had wronged her. I thought that if she couldn't find fault in Jack for his actions, at least she should expect Jack to be helpful to her in remuneration—take out her cans, spend time in her garden, fix her things.

"Well, I'm sorry all the same, Agnes," I said. "I'll keep an eye on him from now on. And I will send him over to help you with whatever you need."

"Oh, I'd like that," she said in singsong.

The boys returned before too long, but without their father. Another scotch worked its magic; my mood cooled. I daydreamed wistfully about Jack. I began making the place presentable. There was a horrible ant problem in the kitchen. I sent the boys into town on their bicycles with a list of things to buy. Milk, eggs, flour, sugar, cranberries, some items for Mrs. Steeves, and insecticide.

"Oh Jack," I sighed. I made up the bedroom and straightened out the boys' room. I'd stayed in the house only a few times. It was beautiful, but I resented its existence. Jack summered on the island growing up. We used to take vacation rentals there as a young family. He bought the house a few years prior, at the start of his mid-life crisis, just before he ran off with Eva Braun. I lay on the bed smoking a cigarette and enjoying the fresh sea breezes.

I reformulated my plans. I would collect the money and then I'd win Jack back. We would rekindle the marriage and I could stop worrying about my future, money, and the boys. I would make Jack love me again. I just needed to talk to him. I fell asleep, anticipating being in Jack's arms again.

A noise downstairs woke me; the boys had returned. I went down to the kitchen and started on a cranberry cake for Jack—his favorite. Preparing food was difficult because the kitchen was a mess. The provisions in the pantry—fruit, crackers, cereal—all had ants picking at them. I stabbed or scooped each item into the garbage and spilled undiluted insecticide after it. I took all of the bad food out to the trash and washed the floor with a mixture of soapy water and insect poison. I made a quick lunch for the boys, poured another cheap scotch and wandered outside into the rose garden to sit on the bench in the afternoon sun. I found myself staring at the ants. *Ants are disgusting—exchanging germs, eating worms.* I went back into the house, mixed another batch of water and poison and soaked the whole area. I relaxed a second time in the flood of dying ants.

I had come to the island to intercept the letter from the banker. Jack had a box at the post office. I reasoned that there must be at least two keys. I had to find all of them so that nobody else could access the box. I went back inside again and rummaged through drawers. I found some invitations for parties I wasn't invited to. I found a couple of Deutsch Marks. Behind the door, I found too many keys on eyehooks.

Why does anyone need so many keys?

I pulled them all off and swept them into a Crown Royal bag I'd found in a drawer, wondering at the same time where the Crown Royal might be stashed. I took anything that looked remotely like a car key as well. I tugged the jangling bag out to Jack's car and tried practically every key, except those that were obviously wrong. None of them fit the ignition.

I wondered why, with so many useless keys, Jack didn't keep a car key behind the door too. Sitting sideways in the driver's seat in the growing heat, I kicked the car door wide open and marched down the hill toward the post office. On arriving, I paused to catch my breath in the heat. I stood at the front door looking over the posters to see what was happening on the island. On the left side there were *Wanted* bulletins, but none warned of Jack or his gold-digging German whore. On the right was a poster challenging the neighbors to decorate for the Fourth of July. That sounded like a good activity for me, Mark and John. The prize was a pie by Mrs. Steeves.

I located the Smith post office box by name and spilled the keys onto the corner of the adjoining counter. There were so many keys that the final few slid off the mound and into the crack between the counter and the rack of post office boxes.

"Shit," I muttered. I bent down sideways to see how many had gotten away and where they had gone.

"Martha?"

I stood up and turned to see one of Jack's friends whose name I couldn't recall—a balding man with a large nose.

"Oh, how are you?" I asked.

"What are you doing here? Down to see the boys? You picked the perfect weather," he said.

"Yes, yes" I said, distracted and wishing he would go away, "Nice weather."

There was a moment where nobody said anything, so I piped back in. "I have to send a letter," I said, trying to guard the sight of the pyramid of keys behind my frame. He craned his neck to see.

"It's very nice to see you. I bet the boys are excited."

"Yes, it's nice to be back," I said.

"Hope to see you around."

I wondered if this loser would ever shut up. Finally, he left the post office.

This won't do, I thought to myself. *I can't be caught intercepting the mail. I have to find the right key and think of some other way of checking the box each day.*

I picked through the keys and found one—the right one! I pulled a handful of circulars from the box, scraped the mound of keys into my purse and headed back to the house. There was still no sign of Jack. I hung all of the mystery keys back onto the eyehooks and hid the post-office-box key in the sugar canister.

The afternoon waned but Jack didn't appear. I picked through the garden. Bleeding hearts wilted beneath blooming irises. The strawberries were in. The rhubarb was still wet with dew. I stopped to look at a lily. The nice old woman who lived next door called out to me from the street. I fixed on her withered form.

My God, can she still be alive?

"You know—," she wheezed up to me, "you should water your flowers in the evening." She approached the edge of the property.

"Sorry?"

"You should water in the evening," she said.

"Thank you. I'll take your advice."

She squinted and looked hard at me. "Oh, it's you. I'm glad you're here. Your children need you."

"Aw, that's sweet." I still couldn't recall her name.

"I heard that you scolded my granddaughter for spying."

I was at a loss for words.

"She deserved it," she said, turning to resume her slow shuffling walk before she'd finished speaking.

"Thank you," I said, too quietly to her bent, departing form to be heard. "It is nice to be back." She made me feel good.

I went into the house through the porch door and encountered Mark and John coming through the kitchen with their chubby friend, Nicky.

"Hi, Mrs. Smith," Nicky said, brightly.

"Nick?" I called to him, making him turn and look back. "Would you ask your little sister to come and see me today? I have a job for her."

"What's the job?" asked John.

"It's a woman's thing," I told him. I needed someone to fetch the mail for me each morning so I wouldn't be seen at the post office, but I couldn't let the boys know that.

"What's your sister's name ag—?" I asked Nick, but Mark responded before I could finish the question.

"Patty," he said.

"Fatty Patty!" added John.

Nick punched him in the arm and a game of tag erupted and spilled through the dining room on its way up the main stairway.

"Nick!" I called after them. The whole line stopped and fell back, "Go home and get your sister for me."

"Mom—," whined John.

"Now!"

Nicky trudged back down and the other two followed him out the door. By the time they'd reached the edge of the hill they had regained their bounce and hurried off toward Nicky's.

I dozed off in the master bedroom again, taking in the summer sounds through the open screens. There was a knock on the porch door, downstairs. I jumped up. *It's her. The Nazi!* I stumbled down the steps. Rounding the corner, I could see a woman and a young girl standing on the porch. The woman looked familiar.

"Can I help you?" I asked.

"I'm sorry, were you napping?"

"Oh no," I said, picking my hair. "I was just reading."

There was a pause, and then she spoke again.

"I'm Donna Grimaldi. And this is my daughter Patty."

"Oh, of course," I said. "I know who you are. How are you? It's so nice to see you again. Hi, Patty."

"Nick said you had a job for me?" Her freckled cheeks framed a semi-toothy grin. A pair of big blue eyes fixed on me.

I couldn't give her the task of sneaking the mail—not with her mother standing there.

"I *do* have a job for you," I said to her, thinking quickly of an alternative. "I want you to help me pick and arrange flowers."

Her face brightened even further.

"Come in," I went on. "Would you like a piece of cranberry cake?"

"Sure!" she said.

"Donna? A cup of tea?"

"That would be very nice," Donna said. The two of them stepped into the house. "I haven't seen much of you lately."

"Jack and I have been separated. But we'll be getting back together," I told her.

"Oh, how nice. It will be good to have you around again. Are you staying the summer?"

"Part of it, yes."

Donna mused about the happenings around the beach as I prepared our tea. She hadn't heard about the incident with Jack, Mrs. Steeves' and the garbage cans yet, so I related a softened version.

"Well, people make mistakes," Donna said.

"What's this?" asked Patty, picking at the cranberry glaze.

"Icing," I replied.

"The icing on the cake," said Donna, trying to be funny. She made the interjection so soon after the story of Jack and Mrs. Steeves that it sounded like commentary. Then, to me in feigned confidence, as though Patty sitting beside her wouldn't be able to hear: "The rumor is that Chloe Truesdale is trying to hook your husband."

"Who's that? Is that a German name?"

"I don't think so. She's the local tramp. Nobody can stand her."

"Have you seen a German woman here?"

"No, but I know who you're talking about. She was hanging around Jack last summer. I haven't seen her this year, though I haven't seen Jack yet either."

"Is she a fat woman?" I asked.

"No. Not at all. She's quite pretty."

Imagining Jack with anyone—especially someone attractive— made the bile rise, so I switched subjects: "Tell me more about this Chloe Truesdale."

Donna's eyes lit up as she told me all about Chloe Truesdale's broken life. And while she was at it, she shared some dirt about the pudgy woman next door, Janet. After tea, Patty, Donna and I stepped outside into the late afternoon sunshine.

"Come along, Patty," I said. Donna and I strolled through the flowers, deciding what would go best together. "Clip a couple dozen of those," I said to Patty. "And get a bunch of these."

Patty worked the flowers like a bumblebee. Donna and I searched the shed for old jars and vases. The three of us met up in the kitchen to form an assembly line, cleaning glassware and stuffing it with flowers. By the time we had finished, we'd left very little blooming in the garden and very few containers of any use in the shed.

It was almost dinnertime. I started to worry about the boys. "I'll drive you home," I said.

"We can walk," said Donna.

"Are you sure?" I remembered that I had no car keys anyway.

"I'm too tired to walk home, Mom," Patty whined.

"Oh, okay, honey. I guess we will take that ride, Martha, if you don't mind."

I slipped behind the door to the shrine of keys, flipping through a few of them fruitlessly.

"Say, I have an idea. Take a vase and come with me," I said to Patty.

The three of us crossed the yard to Mrs. Steeves' with a portion of the cranberry cake and a vase of flowers.

"Oh, they're absolutely lovely," said Mrs. Steeves' at the door.

"Agnes, may we borrow your car briefly? We have to get Patty home," I said.

"Certainly, you may borrow my car. But Martha, do you mind if Allison and I come along for the ride? I'm feeling a little cooped up in here, and my shoulder is much better than I thought it would be."

"The more the merrier!" I said. I was delighted to have Agnes along.

So, Donna, Patty and I loaded all of the vases and jars into the back of Mrs. Steeves' station wagon. The five of us drove past the Crescent Club and up the road a half-mile to the Grimaldi's. We found the boys there.

"Will you stay for dinner?" asked Donna's husband, John.

I was anxious to get home; I wanted to wait for Jack and get back to the scotch. Before I could make an excuse, Mrs. Steeves walked into the living room with a glass of Irish.

"Oh! Do you have any scotch?" I asked.

John Grimaldi produced a full bottle of single-malt. Heaven. "What will you do with the flowers?" asked John.

"Well, I thought we might deliver them to some of our neighbors," I said. It was the first time I'd thought about it. "We could deliver them after dinner. Wouldn't that be fun?"

And so, following a simple summer meal, that's what we did: John, Mark, Patty, Nick, Donna, Mrs. Steeves and Mrs. Steeves' lovely niece Allison and I all crowded into her station wagon. We bounced down the shore road laughing and arguing about who should deliver the next vase of flowers and who wanted ice cream. In a short while, we gathered other families in other cars. Eventually, the whole group of us—must have been twenty or so—gathered at the Crescent Club for a fire on the beach, marshmallows and songs. The boys took to Mrs. Steeves' niece. What a wonderful evening! Everyone was happy to see me. It felt good to be back.

Unfortunately, Jack didn't come home that night. I needed him. I needed the money. I thought that it might all work out if I could just talk to him.

{ LARRY PULJCISZ }

Tuesday, July 2nd

I'm an undertaker. I spent summers on the island, growing up. Jack was one of my friends. I always envied him; he was good-looking; he was successful. I got dealt a long beak and a bald patch that struck me in my early twenties. He got the girls. I do okay, but I get dead girls mostly. Undertaker humor.

I was walking along the rocks back from town with the morning paper and mail for my mom. I saw Jack coming from the other direction.

"Larry, I haven't seen you in years," Jack said. "What's new?"

"Nothing much," I said. "I'm visiting with my mom."

"Are you married? Do you have any kids?"

"Nah," I said, squinting against the sun to look into Jack's eyes. "I never found Miss Right. Well, a couple times I did, but by then she'd passed on."

Jack chuckled at that one.

"How about you? I heard that you and Martha were back together."

"Back together? No way. The divorce is in the works."

"What happened to the foreign girl I heard about from last summer?"

"The German— oh, she ditched me for the next guy that came along." Jack's voice weakened a little when he said that. "But I've got a problem," he continued. "Martha is here, and she's not supposed to be."

"Where is she supposed to be?" I asked.

"Your office," he laughed and then continued more seriously: "Well, back in Hartford maybe, but definitely not here. The judge told her to stay away."

"I saw her yesterday," I said, "at the post office."

"You saw her? What did she say?"

"She didn't know who I was, but she said you two were back together, or something like that. Why don't you just tell her to leave?"

"I can't. She's the boys' mother. I can't be throwing their mother out. At least not again."

At that moment, a boat making its way across the bay stole Jack's attention. A small sailboat tagged along behind it, in tow.

"Finally," Jack exclaimed, gesturing to the boats. He turned to me: "C'mon, my boat is here. Let's take her for a sail."

"Well, I gotta bring the mail to my mom," I said. "And then have lunch with her. But I can come back out while she takes her nap."

Jack scowled for an instant and then lightened up again as something else caught his eye. Up the beach, a slender girl made her way along the rocks, stepping from one to another with arms extended as if walking a tightrope. She was tall, thin and young, wearing pink hot pants and a light blue top. Straight dirty blonde hair hid her face as she conjured a path through the maze of slippery rocks. Jack stood transfixed. The boats slid by behind him, forgotten.

"Is that Laurie Johnson?" he whispered.

"I think it is," I said. "She's grown into a beautiful girl."

"My God," he said.

Jack was twenty-five years too old for her, but he mumbled some things that suggested he thought she might be in reach. She neared us, looked up and smiled. A foot slipped. She stumbled, recovered and giggled. Jack lunged to save her anyway, letting go of her arm only when it was well past obvious that she had regained her footing. She beamed.

"Mr. Smith, how are ya?" She turned to me and said a simple, "Hello."

"Larry," I said. "Call me Larry."

"Hello," she repeated.

Her blue shirt bore the seal of the volunteer fire department, folded over her bountiful chest.

"You're with the fire department?" I asked. Jack stared at the emblem.

"Oh, yeah! It's really far out. We have the greatest crew."

"Do you go on fire calls?" asked Jack. "Do you ride the fire truck?"

"Oh, sure. Well, there hasn't been a fire yet, but I will."

Jack looked up from her shirt. "Are you trained?"

"Not yet. But the guys are having me pull hoses. I think I'm kind of their mascot, maybe. But I'm serious about it."

Laurie changed the subject, addressing Jack specifically: "Are you down for the entire summer?"

"Yes," he said, "we're here for the duration."

"Is Katrin here?"

"Well, no," he said. "We kind of broke up."

"Oh, I'm sorry. I really liked her."

"Yeah," said Jack with a sigh. He looked up to see if he was going to get any more pity from Laurie, but as soon as he made eye contact she flashed a big grin and said: "Well, it was really nice to see you. I'm on my way to the club. Say 'hi' to the boys for me. If you need me to babysit, let me know."

"Okay thanks, Laurie," said Jack. "Goodbye."

I added my goodbye: "Goodbye, Laurie."

"Yeah," she said flatly.

"Larry," I reminded her.

"Yep." She began making her way along the rocks toward the Crescent Club. Jack watched her for a moment or two and then turned back to me.

"Well, how about this afternoon? Want to go sailing?"

"This afternoon is okay. Can I come by your house at about one?" I asked.

"No. I can't go there," Jack said with a pained expression. "That brings up a problem. How am I going to get my sails?"

"Where are they?"

"They're in the shed. But I can't go there with Martha around."

"You can't stay away forever," I suggested.

"Yeah, but—" Jack considered his options. "Will you get them for me?"

"She can't be that bad. Does she bite?"

"Absolutely. But the real problem is that I just don't know what to say to her yet. I know I'll have to face her eventually."

"Okay," I said. "Tell me what to look for."

Just before one o'clock, I walked up the hill to Jack's house and made my way around the back to the shed. I pulled a sail bag out from beneath the things that had settled upon it. It took a good deal of tugging, and junk fell from the shelves on either side. A good hearty yank finally freed the bag. I fell back slightly. Two hands touched my shoulders.

"Ah!" I screamed, not expecting anyone behind me. I turned to find myself face-to-face with Jack's wife. "Martha! I was just—"

"You're the fellow who was in the post office yesterday morning," she said. "Have you seen Jack?"

I was unprepared to answer the question. "It's a sail bag," I blurted out. "My name is Larry." I offered a trembling hand. She took it and pumped it gently as if it were a lever of some kind. Her grasp was soft and warm, unlike most of the hands I touch. Her countenance was entrancing.

"Hello, Larry," she continued. "Where is Jack?"

"I— I saw him this morning," I confessed. Her perfume spoke to me. She surveyed me in silence for a moment.

"Well then, let's chat. Come inside for a cup of tea."

She gave me a tug by the collar, turned me bodily and steered me toward the house. Hands on my back led me to the screen door, through the kitchen and onto the porch. Her touch sent shivers through me.

The view from the porch was magnificent. Martha and I sat overlooking the summer scene below—the bay, the Crescent Club and the ferry dock. I looked at the woodwork of the house and imagined what it would be like to live there, especially with someone like her.

"Milk and honey, Larry?" she asked as she brought out the tea.

"Yes, thank you," I replied from my dream.

Martha had been painting the millwork on the porch columns in red, white and blue, alternating bands of color. Three cans of paint sat open, each with its own brush submerged past the bristles. The peeling grey deck paint was covered in patriotic drips and spatters. I think she read the horror in my face as I took in the mess.

"It's not a big deal," she said. "The porch needs painting anyway. So, tell me what's going on with Jack."

I wanted to engage her. The problem was that I really didn't know anything.

"We're going sailing," I offered.

"C'mon!" she searched for my name, but went on without it: "Is he seeing anyone?"

"Well, I don't—"

"Is he still seeing that German whore?"

"Oh, no," I said authoritatively. "She dumped him."

"Ha!" she said, followed by a pause. Then, in staccato: "I'd heard that. But I'm not sure whether to believe it. Does he still talk to her? Does she still come here?"

"Well, I'm not sure—" I started.

"Who is Chloe Truesdale?" she barged in.

Suddenly, I was lost. What did Chloe have to do with anything? She had not, to my knowledge, been involved with Jack lately. Though, I heard she'd brought him dinner the other night, so maybe. But then, I also heard that Jack was flirting with Elizabeth.

"Chloe Truesdale? Chloe is someone we grew up with," I said.

A woman's voice sang "Yoo-hoo?" from within the house. Mrs. Steeves worked her way through the kitchen. She stepped out through the porch door with a measuring cup in hand. "Martha, dear, do you have any sugar?"

Her voice became deadpan when she saw me.

"Oh, you have company."

There was no hint of recognition, even though I was the one who had embalmed and buried her husband.

"I'm Larry. Larry Puljcisz," I said.

"That's right. How is your mother?"

Before I could answer she muttered "Oh, my," as she took in the disastrous painting project.

Martha stood behind me and off to one side. Her hand gently touched the back of my arm to ask that I let her pass. Her perfume mixed with female sweat, the smell of hydrangea, paint and the sea breeze. Her breast brushed me. I watched her curves as she passed by.

"What do you need, Agnes?" Martha asked.

"I was hoping to borrow a cup of sugar, dear."

"Of course. It's on the counter in the canister. Help yourself."

"Oh, and to be a total pest, is your rhubarb in? Can you spare any?"

"Oh, I wouldn't know, Agnes," Martha said. "But you are certainly welcome to it if you find it. How's your shoulder?"

"Actually, I haven't felt this good in years," she giggled as she descended the steps on her way to the garden. She flashed a suspicious glance back at the red, white and blue mess. Then at me.

I'd forgotten the time! Jack would be wondering what had happened to me. But I was conflicted: I would rather spend time on with Martha than sail with Jack. At the same time, I didn't want Jack to appear here—not now—when I was having feelings for his wife.

"I have to go," I said.

Martha turned, cupped my hand and put her lips to my ear: "Tell Jack to come home. I just want to talk," she whispered.

"Anything," I whispered back, taking a deep draught of the fragrance of her hair.

The sail bag hanging over my shoulder beat me on the ass with every step down the hill, as if to hasten me away from there. I found Jack sitting bored on the Crescent Club porch.

"What happened to you? You see a ghost?" he asked upon seeing me.

"I saw Martha," I gasped.

"That's almost as bad. What did she say? Why is she here?" he asked.

"I only saw her for a moment or two," I lied. Then, finding a little bit of courage to come to her defense: "She seems really nice."

"Ach!" he said. "She's psychotic."

I didn't want to pick sides, but it seemed to me that Jack might be the one to blame—running with loose women and getting drunk in public. I bit my lip. Really, it was good to have someone to hang around with while I was visiting my mom.

"She just wants to talk to you," I offered.

Jack didn't respond. "Let's get out there," he said. "I think I feel a breeze."

I was surprised and relieved that Jack didn't probe further about my visit with Martha. We rode the launch boat to the mooring where the newly-arrived sailboat bobbed low in the water. Standing beside me in the cockpit, Jack looked perplexed as he surveyed the rigging.

"It's funny," he mused. "I thought I remembered that cleat being made of brass. I had this same issue on Liz's boat the other day. After a long winter, I've forgotten some of the details of my own— What the fuck is that?"

Peering into the bilge water, Jack bent over and plucked out a crucifix. He turned and flung it into the bay with such enmity that I looked about for the thunderbolt that would kill us.

"God, what's wrong with people anyway?" he muttered.

Jesus went *bloip* as he hit the water. I would have thought it was funny if I weren't afraid of going to hell. I couldn't imagine the reason for Jack's reaction.

"Where'd that come from?" he demanded of me.

"I have no idea," I said.

Without Jesus in the boat, the wind and chop picked up considerably. I never was a sailor, so I was almost useless to Jack. He was a little gruff sometimes when I asked a stupid question or grabbed the wrong rope. The boat was leaky. Jack said that the leaking would stop in a week or so, once the planks had swelled up. So, while Jack sailed, I bailed. We ran out of things to say pretty quickly, and Jack seemed edgy. Finally, I introduced the questions that Martha had asked me—at the same time sucking out water with the bilge pump so as not to look overly interested:

"Are you seeing Chloe?" I asked.

"What? Who said that?"

"Oh, nobody," I said. "I just thought you might..."

"She's nice. But she's not my type. Say two kind words to her and she's picking out a china pattern."

"Does the German girl ever come around?"

"Huh? Nah. I told you, she dumped me—no contact. I don't want anything to do with her."

"You see much of Liz?"

"What's with all the questions?"

"Oh, it's nothing," I said. "I've always lived vicariously through you."

He looked satisfied with that and chuckled. I wondered that he might be sleeping with all of them.

"Larry," Jack asked when we'd gotten back to the mooring and secured the boat. "Do you want to race this weekend?"

"I'll ask my mom if she's got any plans for us."

This made Jack scowl again.

It was the middle of the afternoon. Though I had no business, I wanted to stop in to see Martha again. I needed to be sure that Jack wasn't heading home.

"Are you going home now?" I asked.

"Nah. I'm not ready to face Martha yet. I'm going to let her stew a while."

"Want me to bring the sails back?"

"Sure. Are you coming back down here?"

"No, I have to get dinner ready for Mom."

He gave me yet another disparaging look and I started to get mad, but I choked it back down. "What are you doing tomorrow?"

"I thought I'd like to go fishing with the boys in the morning, if I can get word to them," he said. "Do you want to come with us?"

"Sure. Nine o'clock?"

"Sounds good," he said.

"What are you going to do now?" I asked again to make sure Jack wasn't going home.

"I dunno. Probably hang out at the club."

When I got to Jack's house, it was nearly four o'clock. I made as much noise in the shed as I could. Martha didn't appear, so I heaved the wet sail bag into the dark shed and headed for the house. I gave the back kitchen screen door a gentle rap, heard nothing and peered in.

"Hello there, Larry," came a sultry voice.

She'd been expecting me! I cracked the door and slid in. Through the opposite screen door, I could just make out the feet of one of the boys, kneeling as he set up lines of dominoes around the corner of the porch. I tried to draw their mother out of the boys' eyeshot—against the odd chance there could be a kiss. She approached me playfully, smiling, placing both hands open-palmed on my chest, letting them slide down slowly.

"Care for a shot, Larry?"

Her breath was ripe with scotch. It was sweeter than the

formaldehyde smell of most women I get close to. "Sure," I gasped, and then was surprised when she simply handed me the bottle. I took a sip and shuddered at the taste, not being very well acquainted with liquor. She came very close and stared slightly cross-eyed into my eyes. I pursed my lips to kiss her.

"Mom?" came a child's voice through the porch screen door. I backed away, breathless—caught! Martha simply turned and composed herself.

"What is it, dear?" she asked.

He dropped his question when he saw me. "Never mind." He disappeared back onto the porch and then in retreat down the front steps with his brother. I wanted to go with them. And I wanted to stay with Martha, too. She turned back toward me and made another approach. I retreated, backing into the refrigerator. She pinned me there with her torso.

"Care for another, Larry?"

A charge of panicked excitement raced through me. I was nervous that the boys would return, or that Jack would come home, or that a neighbor would arrive unannounced. I wanted to get Martha someplace safer—like the bedroom. But I didn't want to lose this moment. As I raised my hands to cup her head for a captive kiss, one of my fears became real:

"Can you help me light the fire?" It was the scraping voice of an old woman outside the back kitchen door.

"Ugh," I groaned, sliding sideways from between Martha and her appliances. Martha braced her gentle fall into the refrigerator with her palms.

"Yes, Lilly. What's the matter?" Martha said to the unseen specter beyond the door. Her demeanor was so nonchalant that I found it frightening; I was near trembling; she had switched gears as though nothing had transpired.

"I can never light this grill. I can never tell whether the gas is on or off," returned the lizardly voice.

"Oh, dear. You could blow up the house. Larry," said Martha turning to me. "Would you light Lilly's fire?"

I froze. Until now, the old woman hadn't known I was there. I wasn't ready to walk without adjusting myself, and I couldn't adjust myself with the both of them eyeing me.

"Larry?" she repeated with a little more song in her voice, "Help Lilly, would you dear? The gas could cause an explosion."

She called me *dear!*

"Of course," I gasped and slid out the back door into the service of the ancient hag waiting beyond. I was sure I'd buried this woman the year before. I followed her shuffling figure through the roses, through an opening in a barnyard fence to a grill in the narrow space between Martha's house and hers. The open grill hissed. The whole area smelled of gas.

"Jesus! Can't you hear that? Can't you smell that?" I asked, searching in a panic for the shutoff. "Don't light anything for ten minutes," I barked at her.

She ignored me, instead sampling a cold, uncooked hot dog from the grill. "Mmmmm," she said.

A man stepped out of the cottage onto the side porch to see what the commotion was about. "Who's this?" he asked Lilly.

Lilly looked at me and then at the man, and shrugged her shoulders.

"My name is Larry," I said.

An overweight woman joined him in on the porch. "Who's that?" she asked the man.

"Martha Smith suggested I help Lilly with the grill," I said to the pair.

"I knew it! That's Martha Smith who's staying next door," said the overweight woman.

"What's wrong with the grill?" the man asked, suspiciously.

An older, gaunt woman joined them on the porch. "What's going on, Frank?" she asked the man.

"This guy's screwing with our grill."

Lilly gazed at me, but didn't offer any defense.

"Who are you?" demanded the woman in a shrill voice. "Lilly, what's going on?"

"What's happening, Janet?" asked a third woman upon entering the porch.

"Martha Smith is staying next door. She's the one who threw the bag at me," she said.

"He's messing with the grill," said Frank.

A skinny fellow in a t-shirt joined them. "Hey, that's the undertaker," he said. "What's he doing here?"

"He's bothering Lilly," said the gaunt woman.

"Hey, undertaker! She's not quite dead yet."

The whole group laughed heartily.

I beat a retreat. I ran back through the fence to Martha's house. She wasn't in the kitchen any longer. I tiptoed upstairs to the master bedroom, hoping she'd be there. I went through the upstairs porch door and looked out over the railing. Then, I saw Jack walking up the hill and toward the house. I nearly fell down the stairs trying to escape. I ran out the back door and around the side of the house, past Lilly, down the side yard and into the woods. I could smell the gas and hear the grill hissing again as I raced by.

I emerged a muddy escapee on the far side of the woods. I took a deep breath and composed myself so that my mother wouldn't ask any questions. When I reached her house, I found that she had a visitor. From behind, I thought it was Cap'n Bob. It seemed odd that he should be here, but I wasn't about to question my mother's business.

"Hello," I said, timidly. The two of them sat uncomfortably across a plate of crackers in the living room. The visitor stood up from a creaking chair and turned to shake my hand. It wasn't Cap'n Bob at all. It was father Ivan. He was in street clothes.

"You know we're having a church picnic—" he began.

"Where have you been?" Mom cut him off.

"The beach," I said.

"How did you get your shoes so muddy?"

I looked down at my shoes and stepped back. I'd crossed the threshold onto mom's Oriental rug with muddy shoes. There would be an inquisition.

"I took the shortcut through the woods," I said.

"From the beach?" She'd found a hole in my story already.

"No, Mom. I stopped at Jack Smith's house."

Her tone began to sharpen: "Was Martha there too?"

"Well—," said Father Ivan at the increasing cadence of doubt. "I must be going." He picked up a check from the coffee table and headed for the front door. Mom let me off the hook for the moment and followed him.

"Good evening, Father, and thank you for stopping by," she said sweetly.

Father Ivan turned to me. "You should come by the church more often."

"That is a grand idea," mother said.

"In fact, we're a having a picnic on Thursday. You could come help out," he said.

I was to race with Jack on Thursday. "The Fourth? I've got a commitment, Father."

"Nonsense, Lawrence," said Mom. "The church comes first." Then to Father Ivan: "He'll be there."

Father Ivan looked back at me to be sure I'd understood and acknowledged the dictate.

"Well, good evening, Doris. And to you too, young Mr.—," he looked at the check in his hand, searching for help pronouncing our last name. It came out "Pulljicks." The door shut behind the priest and the smell of mothballs reemerged from the cracks like tendrils of demons. I looked for something to say.

"I thought that was Cap'n Bob. I've never seen Father Ivan out of his priest garb before."

"Of course you have," Mother said. "Though, he and his brother do look alike."

"But they don't get along at all," I added.

Something woke me that night; I smelled smoke. I stared out into the darkness. Through the canopy of trees, over on the far side of the woods, I glimpsed the dance of a wall of flames. A campfire! I strained to hear joyful noises through the still night air. Houses lined the street on the far side of the woods; it could be anyone's celebration. I leaned on the sill for an hour, listening for one laugh, one happy shriek that I could identify as Martha's.

"Oh, Martha," I said under my breath. *Martha.* I was worried that Martha and Jack might have fallen into each other's arms. I was hopeful that they'd reached another impasse—another opportunity for me. *Which flames were being fanned now?*

I wanted to be sleeping and oblivious. At the same time, I wanted to run out into the summer night air and experience what life felt like—I was so well acquainted with death. Mother's door creaked on her way to the bathroom. I snuck back into bed, lest she discover me awake.

Wednesday, July 3rd

The next morning, I went to the post office to fetch the mail for mother. Martha was there again. She squatted below the counter, suspended by an arm, looking for something beneath the rack of post office boxes. A small cotton bag full of keys sat on the surface above her. I tipped my head sideways to see what she was reaching for and spied the glint of a few of the keys she'd spilled the day before. She squatted deeper in her white cotton skirt and stretched to reach the keys. I circled around behind her, unconsciously reaching out to touch her bottom and then pulling my hand back as I realized what I was doing. I was afraid of all that might have transpired between her and Jack last evening. I wanted to engage her. I wanted reassurance. I wanted Martha.

"Hello? Martha?" I asked meekly.

"Damn it," she muttered as she stretched an arm into the dusty space below the boxes.

"Do you need help?" I asked, speaking a little louder.

"I'm trying to reach these goddamned keys!" she said, still not looking up to see that it was me.

"Here, let me help you," I offered.

She eased her way out. Sitting on her ankles, she looked up to me and said: "Oh, Harry. Thanks. I can't reach them. They're under there."

Harry? Who was *Harry?* I squinted and regained my composure. I got down on my knees and muttered a few words about lost keys and then turned, suddenly finding myself face-to-face with Martha under the post office counter in a room full of comings and goings. We were so close. She smelled like fresh laundry. I closed my eyes and leaned into her to steal a kiss. She recoiled in surprise, banging the back of her head into a bolt securing the heavy wooden table leg. The bag of keys above spilled its contents off the counter like a Slinky uncoiling off the edge of a step. The cascade of metal was frighteningly loud under the circumstances. Martha's eyes squeezed tightly from the pain, forming asterisks.

"Fuck!" she shouted.

I gasped and shimmied out from under the table. The postmaster was behind me—tall enough that he was still towering above me, even after I stood up.

"Problem?" he asked.

"She lost her key," I replied.

"She seems to have plenty," he said, nodding to the mess on the floor.

"It's not a problem," Martha croaked from under the table. "I dropped my box key. It's here. No big deal."

"Well, okay," said the postmaster, walking away.

I crawled back beneath the counter on my knees. Martha smelled like a whole laundromat full of clean laundry. She rubbed the back of her head and looked for blood on her hand. Not finding any, she reached out and touched my side.

"Harry," she said, "did you find a key in the sugar bowl? There has to be another one here somewhere."

I could smell her soft breath—like a spoonful of Rum Raisin.

"What sugar bowl?"

"Did-you-find-a-key-in-my-sugar-bowl?" She spelled it out as if I were an idiot.

"You mean another one?" I asked. She looked frustrated. I asked myself how many keys one person needs.

"Never mind. Just help me clean these up," she directed.

She left the post office with a cotton bag full of keys, dust bunnies and beach sand. My heart sank.

I arrived at Mom's house with the morning paper. Two fishing rods leaned by the front door.

"Mom?"

"Inside," she sang out. I swung the door into the mothballed air, letting the morning sunlight take a bite out of the gloom. Jack sat captive in a low chair with his knees above his hips. A paper-thin china cup and saucer occupied his hands.

"Larry!" he blurted happily, as if I were the bailiff. "We're doing a little fishing, right?" He put down the coffee and extracted himself from the chair.

"Where are the boys?" I asked.

"Well, they wanted to spend time with their mother."

Mom's face lit up. "Oh, I heard that you and Martha got back together."

Jack steeled himself and then addressed the coffee table, gently slicing a stiff hand through a vertical plain as though giving a benediction. "Martha is here to see the boys for a few days. Then she is returning home."

I was relieved that Jack didn't want Martha. At the same time, I began to think that she might be a little difficult to deal with— certainly more difficult than the girls in my shop.

"That's a shame," Mom said. "She's such a nice girl."

Jack growled and my mother rolled her eyes. Jack took this as his cue to wait outside. I searched the back closet for fishing gear. Mother stood behind me the whole time, arms folded.

"I don't know how I feel about you spending time with that Jack Smith. I've been hearing stories. I wouldn't want you making the same mistakes," she said.

I thought of Martha. "Mom, we're just going fishing."

"Will there be any girls?"

"Mom, I'm forty-three years old!"

She regrouped for a moment. I rummaged for my dad's tackle box.

"Why don't you ask that nice Elizabeth on a date," she said.

"She's Jack's friend."

"Well, just because someone knows Jack—that doesn't mean you can't ask her on a date."

I thought of Martha again. "I'm not attracted to Elizabeth," I said. I knew that Elizabeth would never be attracted to me anyway.

"Why can't you find someone like that nice Polish girl that came to your office last week?"

"Mom, she was *dead!*"

"She wasn't *always* dead."

It was time to go. I abandoned the search for the tackle box and took the most easily extracted fishing rod. I found Jack asleep in the morning sunshine atop mother's wooden front steps.

"Jack?" I prodded him.

"Huh?" he asked, waking up.

"Let's get going."

We gathered the rods and tackle and made our way down to the beach.

"You're tired?" I asked, resigned that he had probably been up all night with Martha.

"I slept on the beach."

"You didn't go home at all?" I wanted to say, *But, I saw you coming up the hill.* That would have given me away.

"I went home to get a few things—a toothbrush, a shirt, deodorant."

"Wasn't Martha there?"

"No. I saw her walking down the shore road. That's how I knew it was safe to go to the house."

I was mulling over whether to admit that I'd seen Martha that morning. When we reached the rocks, I couldn't keep it to myself any longer. "I saw Martha again this morning."

"Where?" Jack asked.

"At the post office."

"That's odd. Twice now," he said.

We walked in silence a while longer, working our way to the end of the jetty where we could sit and fish. Jack laid the fishing rods on the rocks. I found flat spots for a tackle box, a net and a bait trap. We set about looking for mussels or something to place into the bait trap. We threw the trap into the water on a line and then Jack turned to tend to the rods.

"Have you seen her yet?" I asked.

"Hmmm?"

"Martha. Have you seen her?"

"Why all the questions?"

"Just interested," I said. "As I said, I've always lived vicariously through you."

Jack gave me a doubtful frown. He didn't take the bait like yesterday.

"Hmmm," he said, looking at the tackle. He picked up the second rod and ran part of the tackle across his hand. "Interesting. You see this, Larry?" he asked. "This is a post office box key."

I leaned over to look. The last ones to use the rod were Jack's boys. A key had been fixed to the fishing line just above the hook in the spot where one might place a lure.

"Is it your key?" I asked.

"I don't know," he said. "But this sure seems like a coincidence. Let's do some fishing at the post office, shall we?"

Jack lived a charmed life; the key fit. The box had mail in it. He sorted through it, throwing out the junk mail and returning some pieces to the box. One letter caught his attention. He flipped it over, looked at the back and then ran his finger under the flap.

"What the—?" Jack asked as he read it over once, twice, each time becoming more cross. He crumpled the letter, threw it into the wire trash basket and reached for the pay phone. He placed a collect call to one Dennis Burke, loudly enough for me to hear.

"Dennis?" he asked when he finally got through. "What's this all about? Well forget it!" he said. "Send another letter that says—" At that point, he realized that his private business was being aired in public. He cupped the receiver to his mouth and gave instructions that I wasn't able to hear.

"C'mon, let's go," he said after hanging up.

"Everything okay?"

"Yeah. That psycho— I think I know why she's here. Let's go."

Jack pushed his way through the post office door without me. I paused over the trash basket, sifting through the top layer of junk mail and wadded papers looking for the discarded letter. The postmaster came up behind me.

"Lose another key?" he asked.

"A letter from my girlfriend," I said, nervously choosing the most ridiculous lie possible.

He extended a cupped hand and I instinctively opened my palm. He dropped six or seven of Martha's lost keys into the hollow of my hand.

"I hope one of these is the key to her heart," he said, walking away.

Through the front window, I could see Jack waiting for me, scouring the FBI posters and looking none too patient. I found the crumpled letter in the basket, stuffed it into my pocket, and headed for the door.

"Fucking women," Jack huffed.

We descended the steps and walked back up the beach in stony silence. We caught no fish that morning. At one point, Jack looked up at the sky and said: "Well, that's it, I guess." I wondered what he could mean; it seemed a little dire for fishing. But after we parted I got an inkling from the wadded letter:

Dear Jack,

I hope you are having a nice time away.

I thought I had better write you to let you know that your estranged wife was in our office looking for money last week. She instructed me to write you for permission to release funds to her. This is that note. She apparently doesn't know of your financial condition. She seems to think that there is quite a bit of money set aside. As your friend and your banker, I have to tell you that I'm not comfortable being in the middle. Please do me the service of responding with a letter that I can show to her directly.

I hope things turn the corner for you, Jack. At some point this summer, please come to see me so we can plan how to liquidate your assets to cover some of your debts. The only protected property is the beach house, which happens to be in Martha's name, and insured with her as the sole beneficiary. I'll leave it to you to disclose that to her if she isn't already aware.

Sincerely,
Dennis Burke

{ FATHER IVAN }

I'd presided over some awful parishes in the past—Norwich,
Norwalk—any distressed place that began with an "n" in the state
of Connecticut. I'd never been terribly political, so I had to endure a
variety of personally degrading assignments in exchange for a station
I considered fit for myself. It made me cynical. But I was delighted
to have summers on the island again, like when I was a child. During
the off-season, I resided in New London, helping administer to a
mixed flock.

The truth is, even if there were no God, the church would
continue. But if there were no widows with checkbooks, well—God
would be as good as dead. I don't know how many weeks my faith
could have sustained me in a place like New London if nobody came
to the service or the heating oil ran out. But it was my profession.
And I liked to think that it was my duty to help people keep God
alive in various ways, particularly through charitable contribution.

The residents of the island should have spent more time with me and dug a bit deeper into their pockets. It was harder to exercise my authority than it would have been, had I been a newcomer. But the relationships and shared history were irreplaceable. I'd been able to rejoin the Crescent Club. I even bought a small sailboat. I hadn't sailed much as a youngster, but the activity had become so popular that I thought I'd give it a whirl.

In my spare moments, I made it my business to reach out to the island's children to provide them with a positive role model. I had one close male friend, Nil Howard, the local constable. I particularly valued the company of the island women, though I'll admit that I was never attracted to them, except as human beings.

One morning, early in the week, I went to visit Mrs. Puljcisz, a widow living on one of the roads back away from the water. She and I were not very close, but I was well acquainted with her deceased husband. Sometimes she would invite me to her cottage to reminisce about him. Typically, she donated two hundred dollars or so in exchange for an hour of chitchat.

Her son, Lawrence, always hovered like a ghost in the household and around the beach area. He took up undertaking for the island, like his father. In my opinion, he was not particularly capable at the job. Lawrence never had the solemn look one needs as an undertaker. As with priests, people expected a certain demeanor at a funeral. Lawrence always looked as though he were just starting out; he was a little too sweaty. But Lawrence's father, Stephen, and I were a good team. We looked the part. And when we buried someone, we brought in good money. Stephen knew how to put on a good funeral. He passed away just a couple of years ago, and I'd only been shepherding here for three years or so, so we had a ruefully short run. Lawrence buried his father and I performed the service. That was the last time I saw Lawrence—or Stephen for that matter. We brought in less than fifteen hundred dollars. I worked with the competition out of New London since then. I believe Lawrence took to burying heathens.

We had a church outing scheduled for Thursday, the Fourth of

July. It would take place at a pond in the middle of the island. I could
have planned it better, frankly. The timing clashed with Fourth of
July celebrations planned at the Crescent Club, including a boat race
followed by a celebration and fireworks. I wanted to participate in
the race and Constable Howard had agreed to crew for me. I would
need to leave the picnic early to get to the starting line on time. So,
I enlisted the help of Mrs. Peterson, Mrs. Steeves and Jack Smith to
manage the affair while I took my leave.

My brother, Robert, offered to help me ready the boat. But he
talked too much, and we always ended up bickering, so I finished
caulking and painting alone. The boatyard towed the boat out to a
mooring at the beginning of the week. Nil and I made a practice sail
on Tuesday evening.

"What's this?" Nil asked.

"I think it's the jib sheet."

"Jib?"

"The sail in the front of the boat. The jib sheet is the rope that
pulls the jib in. There should be two of them. Look around. Funny.
The boat has no water in it. It was halfway sunk yesterday."

There was very little wind, which was fortunate because we
twisted a couple of the sail clips and couldn't get the mainsail to
go up all the way. We stayed near the beach, and after having some
trouble getting back to the mooring, Nil walked the boat through
waist high eelgrass and then hung his legs over the bow to paddle the
boat back to anchor. We returned to the rectory under early evening
moonlight, damp and a little cranky.

"I'm not certain that we're ready to race," I said. "Maybe I should
have taken my brother's advice."

"Your brother? He's a blowhard," said Nil.

"Perhaps. But he knows how to sail."

"Who else is racing? We'll take 'em all," Nil said.

"Well, John Grimaldi, Roger-something, the fire department boys,
Jack Smith—"

"That asshole. If he so much as cuts us off, I'm going to break
his neck."

"Jack? Well, cutting us off is perfectly permissible in a race, provided he has the right of way."

"There's something seriously wrong with that man—neglecting his kids, drinking, womanizing, beating up old ladies."

"Well, I agree that it will take an act of God to improve his reputation, but he's going to be helping out at the picnic, so he won't be racing anyway."

Nil wasn't the most cerebral person, and sometimes his gruffness grated on me, but I could rely on him for help with church initiatives and as an activity companion. There hadn't been a crime on the island greater than petty vandalism in the last thirty years, so Nil was always on the lookout for a *raison d'etre*. Still, he seemed a little hell-bent on bringing Jack Smith down. It was becoming harder to find people to stand up for Jack. I decided to put Nil on the defensive.

"Have you ever been abroad?" I asked.

"No. I like it here. Why?"

"Travel broadens the mind. It teaches you to see things through others' eyes," I said.

"I see things clearly enough," he said.

"Sometimes we don't see things as clearly as we think."

"Your brother's traveled. Does he see things clearly?"

"That's different. He and I have different views of the world." I lit a cigarette and turned the conversation back to Nil's prejudices against Jack Smith. "Do you suppose that Jack Smith sees himself as the drunken philanderer that you consider him to be?"

"That's what he is," Nil said.

"Nobody considers themselves to be a bad person. Unless they're pathological. I'd wager Jack thinks highly of himself—perhaps so highly that he sometimes fails to see the good in others. I'm certain that he has good intentions. How do you suppose Jack feels about you?"

"It doesn't matter to me. I have a job to do."

"But what if you were wrong about someone? Would you be open to change?"

"Like how?" Nil asked.

"Let me put it another way. Have you ever found that you'd completely misunderstood something you were certain about?"

"I suppose. In high school."

"What did do you do then? Did you reach out with both hands and embrace the change? Grab it by the neck? Or did you tell yourself, slowly, over time, that you were right in the first place?"

"I'm not sure what you're asking. Shake what by the neck?"

"Do you believe in God, Nil?"

"Of course." Nil reached back to the table behind him for the bottle. "Do you want another scotch?"

I nodded. "Speaking of God, did you see a crucifix?"

"It's around your neck."

"No. Another one—in the boat. I left one in the bilge as kind of a blessing. I couldn't find it. It must be there somewhere," I said.

Loretta Peterson and Agnes Steeves stopped by the church in the early morning of the third of July. Loretta had the picnic games planned out, but she was complaining that she hadn't received any help from Jack Smith.

"Okay, okay," I said, "I'll look into it. And I've got Larry Pilljacks to help too. Has anyone lined up grill cooks? Have parishioners signed up for anything?"

"I'll be making a rhubarb pie," Agnes Steeves volunteered with a smile.

"That's grand, but we're going to be woefully short if the parishioners don't come forward," I said.

"My niece can help. Maybe Martha Smith can help too?" suggested Agnes.

"As long as it gets done. Oh, and one more thing: I need to leave the picnic a little early for another commitment. Can you see that you, Jack and master Pulljicks are there to see the picnic through?"

"Yes, Father. We'll see it through," replied Loretta. She pursed her lips in a doubt-filled frown and glared at the chair that Jack wasn't seated in.

"Do you have a parish list, Father?" asked Agnes.

"Sure, Agnes. Follow me," I said.

Loretta Peterson excused herself, and Agnes followed me into the rectory. The list was where I expected to find it, under a sandwich plate and ashtray that Nil and I had left out the night before. A number of large ants had found the plate and were tugging at a crust of bread. Some of the ants were black. Some were red. Two of the black ants were bullying a wounded red ant at the edge of the table. Eventually the group fell off onto the floor and out of sight. I shook the plate out into open window and wiped the ants from my desk with the back of my hand. I crushed the others with the sole of my shoe. Agnes Steeves watched quietly until I looked up at her, satisfied the ant problem had passed.

"God's creatures," I sighed.

"You know," she said. "My shoulder feels fine. Better it's been in years. I think Jack can be forgiven for knocking me down. And I think he's a better man than he's given credit for. He looks after his boys, and he tries to help out. We should give him a chance."

"Well, he'd have to prove himself to me at this point," I said. "And as a priest, I can't just be forgiving people willy-nilly. Let's see if he rises to the occasion with this picnic. At the same time, we can't just let him fail, or the event will fail. Can you look after this?"

"Looking after him would be my pleasure," said Agnes. "I'll talk to his wife. She'll know what to do about the picnic."

During the morning, a few elderly parishioners came by, mostly looking for reassurances that they had contributed enough to secure their places in heaven, which they never quite had. Around noon, Maura Garren, one of the matriarchs of the Crescent Club, stopped into the rectory. She was a woman at an age where she should be giving in addition to tithing. I invited her to have lunch with me to see what she might be willing to donate.

"Do you like tuna?" I asked.

"Father," she said. "I am concerned with the declining morals of our beach community."

"Help yourself to the pickles," I said, placing a plateful in front of her.

"It seems to me that there's too much self-indulgence among us," she went on.

"Would you like a Bloody Mary? A gin and tonic? I'm going to have a glass of the most delightful scotch. You're certainly welcome to that as well."

"Milk is fine," she said, leaning over her bag. She retrieved two milk bottles and set them on the table. "The milkman lost his marbles this morning. He gave me a double order."

"Well, I think we have all the bases covered," I said, selecting a pickle. "Let's indulge."

"What really trouble me are the younger folks," she went on.

"You're from New Britain, right?"

"Yes. St. Methodius's parish," she said. "The teenagers are drinking beer."

"Father Francis is still at St. Methodius?" I asked.

"He's being transferred. He's has been there for twenty years, you know."

"Oh? Is Father Ryan taking is place as pastor?" I asked, a bit surprised.

"Oh no. Didn't you hear? Father Ryan was stabbed in the sacristy by a homeless transient."

"Oh, my!" I exclaimed.

"He'll never offer Mass again."

"What about the visiting priest, Father Justin? Is that his name?"

"He was arrested on some hearsay from the altar boys regarding mischief in the rectory. He'll never say Mass again, either."

"This is all news to me." I was quite concerned.

"Oh, it's all new news. Just in the last few weeks. Father Francis had to be hospitalized for a near-nervous breakdown. The church is in a rough neighborhood. The stabbings pushed him over the edge. They've promised to relocate him. Lord knows he deserves it," Maura said.

The conversation shifted back to doings on the island. By lunch's end, Maura Garren had named all of the troublemakers and settled into a diatribe regarding Jack Smith: "Just last night I saw him sleeping—drunk, no doubt—half-naked on the beach, curled up against the lobster pots. He couldn't even walk up the hill!"

When she finally left, her whole contribution was a twenty-dollar bill, two forgotten jugs of milk and an untouched mound of tuna.

Nil and I took the patrol car up to the lake to look over the setting for the church picnic. We pulled into the empty lot adjoining the picnic area. Nil offered a cigarette and I produced a bottle of scotch from underneath the seat. We enjoyed a bit of each and then made our way up the hill to the grills and picnic tables.

"It's a lovely spot, isn't it?" I said.

"The best," he said. "It wouldn't be the same without you, Father."

"Aw," was all I dared say. I didn't care to wade too deep into conversation with Nil. But Nil looked as if he was waiting for more.

We walked along a path that led away from the picnic area into a lightly wooded section. Finding a pleasant rock to sit upon, we shared another cigarette and a few swigs from the bottle. I squished a number of red ants.

"Do people like me?" asked Nil. This was a very introspective question, coming from him. I took a minute to answer.

"No, Nil. People don't like you," I said. "That's what makes you a good constable."

"I've never had a woman, you know," he said, looking into the woods, sounding hurt and taking another drink from the bottle.

"Neither have I," I said, chuckling.

"I dated Maura Garren once, years ago, before she was married."

"Yes, Nil. You've mentioned that a number of times," I replied. Oddly, Maura Garren had never mentioned it.

"What do women see in someone like Jack Smith?" Nil asked.

This was a surprise turn in the conversation. Nil's late obsession with Jack Smith grated on me. But frankly, I'd asked myself the same question several times and had come to a conclusion: "They like him because he's a bad character. It's human weakness. It's the same reason women aren't attracted to you and me: we're too good; they're not attracted to well-intentioned men."

"Well, I don't think much of women's judgment anyway," Nil said.

"You mustn't say that," I insisted. "Women are God's creatures too. They just make bad choices."

"Maura Garren...," he trailed off.

We both dozed with our backs against the rock in the light summer breeze. I awoke first, groggy and less than ambitious. I worried that we had done nothing to advance the picnic. I considered my helpers—Agnes, Loretta and Jack—and hoped that they could make the event a success.

"C'mon, Nil." I jostled him awake. "We have to get back for happy hour."

I paused at the entrance of the stony cold church. On this beautiful day, I was gripped by the realization that Christianity was more about death than life. Mother Sun warmed my back. Our tortured God hung over the altar in the darkness, earning his salvation through dying. I left him hanging there, choosing a stroll in the warmth of the late day sun. I headed to the post office—first on the road and then along the beach. I doubled back where the beach met the road again.

Sweaty and holding the door for a stranger on the post office steps, I noticed a wanted poster I hadn't seen before. The picture was blurred. The caption simply said *Fat. Shoot on sight!* It was humorous, even if mean-spirited. I stopped chuckling when I spied a second poster—homemade, with a likeness of me, drawn in freehand. It said *Pedophile.* Me? I scraped it from the window and headed toward the counter to have a sharp word with the postmaster. But I paused halfway there, thinking that if I made too much of a fuss it would simply reinforce the accusation.

I turned back toward the post office boxes. My box was completely stuffed. There was the usual foolishness about Peter's Pence and saving pagan savages. There was also a letter from the Norwich diocese. I was already sweating profusely in my black garments, but with this letter in hand, my face surely turned beet red.

The letter instructed that I was being transferred to the Hartford archdiocese and Father Francis' soon-to-be-vacated post in New Britain.

New Britain? I had spent my career working for my current commission and now I was being transferred to the inner circle of hell. With the letter held firmly in two hands, I babbled in profane tongues: "You fucking fuckers! You fuckers fucked with this fucker for the last fucking time, you fucks! Jesus!" A little pause, then: "*Fuck!*"

I looked up. The post office patrons were agape—horrified parishioners and bemused heathens—watching to see what would come next.

"What the fuck are you looking at?"

I stretched my head to the side with a grimace, reached up under my collar, ripped out the white vestigial tab and flung it into an open trashcan.

"We'll see about this," I said under my breath.

The postal patrons parted like the Sea of Galilee.

I sat in the rectory, loosely grasping a glass of Irish. I stared nervously into the floor as Nil rubbed my shoulders. My faith was weakened, but my vow to the church had revived; what else could I do? If She asked me to go, I would have to go. But I hoped to find a way to remain. I would demonstrate that I was indispensible.

"I'll appeal it," I said. "Clearly the bishop has overlooked the good we're doing here. We'll get through the picnic tomorrow. Everyone will have a grand time. Sunday, we'll cash in the good feelings and send an additional offering to Norwich diocese. If we're lucky, an unexpected funeral will sweeten the pot.

"We'll gather signatures for a petition, too. The island is crowded for the holiday. We can collect an overwhelming number of signatures. Maybe we can get some lost souls to rediscover their faith. I'll baptize a Jew if that's what it takes to get the Bishop's mark."

I extended my whiskey to Nil. "Hey, can you put a little water in this?"

Nil took the glass from me and headed toward the sacristy exit to the church hall, on his way to the lavatory sink at the back of the church.

"Nil—" I stopped him. "Just take it from the stoup," I said, motioning toward the holy water.

Nil paused, looked reverently at the holy water and then pushed the glass of spirits into the stoup to gather a little water over the rim. He returned glass to me.

"It's okay. I'm a priest."

Nil chuckled and nodded.

I got up from the chair, glass in hand and walked outside. Nil left to make his rounds. I sat in a bench, sipping the beatified Irish whiskey and taking in the late day warmth—father, sun and holy spirits. I was certain that I could make a case to stay.

{ R O B }

My name is Rob. I'm from New London. I'd just turned seventeen. I landed a summer job as a ferry dockhand, working the island side of the route. It was a pretty decent gig. I got to stay on the island. I got the first crack at the girls coming over on the ferry, and I could ride back to New London for free. The pay wasn't bad either; the money kept me in records and cigarettes.

It was Wednesday afternoon, July third. The ferry was out. The other dockhand, Evan, and I were leaning on the rail, taking a break. I flicked a butt into the water.

"What do you think of Laurie Johnson?" I asked.

"She's okay," Evan responded. "She's kind of a fire jock. Too old for you anyway."

"Yeah, but she's really nice. I like her," I said.

"So, volunteer for the fire department."

I looked at Evan skeptically.

"Why not?" he taunted. "It could be you, her and nine other firemen in a bed—a ten-alarm fire!"

I ignored him, giving my attention over to a pair of boats under sail. Evan was quiet for a moment.

"What about that new girl? Have you met her?" he asked.

"Allison? She practically attacked me," I said.

"Really?" Evan sounded too interested.

"I liked it at first, but then it got creepy."

"What do you mean at *first?*"

I didn't respond.

Evan continued after a moment: "She's supposed to be wacky, you know."

I think that part of the reason for my interest in Laurie Johnson was that after my experiences with Allison, Laurie seemed like the kind of normal, good girl you would want to be with. I didn't tell Evan that up until yesterday I'd been hanging out with Allison. I certainly wasn't going to tell him that I caught her making out with a summer renter and another time with an Italian guy who'd been coming over to the island on his cigarette boat.

"I'm kidding. I never touched her," I said.

"Well, that's good," Evan said. "She's only fifteen."

Fifteen? I felt a second lump in my throat. If she'd blabbed, my reputation would have been ruined. My parents would have killed me.

"Besides, I want a crack at her," Evan added.

Just then, out of the corner of our eyes, we saw a woman walk down the auto ramp toward the ferry landing.

"That's Mrs. Smith," Evan said, pitching his cigarette into the water. "I'm getting out of here."

"Oh, boys?" Mrs. Smith called out in a singsong voice.

Evan slunk off to the toolshed. I jogged up the ramp to meet her.

"Hi," she said. She was a little flushed and out of breath. She smelled like clean laundry. "I want to make an arrangement with you."

I nodded and lifted the clipboard, thinking that she had a passage request.

"No, not that. You see, there's a church picnic tomorrow. My husband's in charge of volunteers to cook and clean up. Only, I don't think he has any."

I looked back at the clipboard.

"I have to work the ferry dock tomorrow," I said.

"Well—" she said, looking around. "I don't see any ferry."

"It's there," I said, pointing at a boat coming toward us on the horizon.

"In any case, you're certainly not working *all* the time."

"We're supposed to clean—"

She cut me off: "How about if my husband were to throw you and your friends a little party tomorrow in exchange for helping out at the church picnic?"

I wished Evan were here for this. "What kind of party?"

"Do you and your friends like beer?"

I wasn't sure how to answer. Here was an adult asking whether my friends and I liked beer.

"I thought we might order a few kegs," she continued.

A "few" kegs was a lot more beer than the occasional six-pack we got our hands on.

"How many kegs do you think you would need in order to round up some volunteers?" she asked.

"Five?" I suggested.

"Five it is. You bring plenty of friends to help and then you can have your beer. Do we have a deal?"

"Yes, ma'am!"

"Now, remember: Mr. Smith is throwing the party, not me. He's the one who found the volunteers. He's the one who's making the picnic a success. He's the one buying the beer. You haven't even spoken with me. Got it?"

"Got it."

Evan came out of hiding after Mrs. Smith left.

"Can you believe it?" I asked. "Mr. Smith is buying us *five* kegs."

"Five kegs? What for?"

"For helping at the picnic tomorrow," I said.

"That's bullshit. What parent would buy us beer?"

"Mrs. Smith just told me so. Mr. Smith is buying beer for anyone who helps out at the picnic," I said.

"No way! When do we get it?" Evan asked.

"At the picnic, I guess."

"I hope it's not Pabst," Evan said.

"Like you know anything about beer. But five kegs—we can't drink five kegs."

"We could sell tickets," he suggested.

"That's a good idea; make some money."

"Girls drink free!" he shouted.

"A kegger on the Fourth!" I shouted after him.

"Decent," Evan seconded.

"But, there aren't even enough people *on the entire island* to drink five kegs," I continued.

"Let's send word over to New London on the next ferry."

"That's it! We'll tell the dock hands on the other side to spread the word."

"Don't tell anyone here, though." I cautioned.

"Just a few?" he asked

"A few," I said. "I didn't know Mr. Smith was so cool."

"He's not cool. He's old," Evan said.

"He's paying for the beer," I said.

"Yeah. Keep him away from your sister, is all," Evan said.

The incoming ferry was packed. We were running a double schedule because of the holiday. The word was that we would run as often as we needed in order to get everyone over to the island and back. I helped Evan unload and hopped the mid-afternoon return ferry to New London to talk to the dockhands on the other side about the party. Evan promised he'd have someone stand in for me with the dock lines when the boat returned.

I couldn't just ride. If I was onboard, I had to work. I checked in with the captain. He sent me to the galley. The cook started in on me immediately. I dragged a wet rag over everything. I moved boxes of number ten cans of tuna, five gallon buckets of soap, the refrigerator. I swamped, mopped and worked the mop through the ringer. My hands were pruney and I smelled like Clorox. I imagined Evan hanging over the rail at the crib dock, pitching his butts in the water.

"Take fifteen minutes," the cook said at last.

I went out on deck. We were five minutes from New London.

"Hey," I said to a girl that I recognized from town. She was sitting alone on a bench. I didn't know her name.

"Katy," she said.

"Do you live on the island?"

"No. I work at the grocery store. I commute on the ferry."

"You want to go to a keg party tomorrow?"

"Well… I'm kinda sick of the ferry."

"Girls drink free. Guys—three dollars."

"Food too?"

"Sure. It's a picnic. Come around noon. Tell everyone you know."

"Alright. I'm going to a big party tonight. I'll tell everyone."

The ferry arrived at the dock in New London. I ran down the gangplank to help unload. Two lines of cars and a mob of people waited for the outgoing trip. A propane truck idled on the side. Commercial vehicles had first dibs on space no matter how many cars were waiting. I backed the truck in. Frank, one of my counterparts from the New London side of the ferry, directed cars in behind the truck.

"Spread the word," I said to Frank. "We're having a kegger at the lake in the afternoon."

"I can't go to a party on the Fourth of July. I gotta work. You gotta work, too."

I hadn't thought about that until now: the New London dockhands would be busy here; they couldn't come. They wouldn't have any interest in spreading the word either. And I especially didn't want to tip them off that Evan and I would be skipping out to go drinking between ferries.

"Yeah, you're right. Have a great Fourth, man," I said.

"I have to work," he grumbled.

We were going to need more beer drinkers. Across the street from the ferry terminal, in the overflow lot, I saw a line of hotrods parked in the sun. Doing the math I figured four people per car, times ten cars, times three bucks—that was one-hundred-twenty bucks right there. I ran up the car ramp, through the lines of waiting cars, out the terminal gate and across the street. I approached the gear-heads. They were a scary bunch, roughly my age. They'd be totally out of place on the island.

"Hey, you guys want to come to a party?"

I gave them the details.

"Are there going to be cops?" one of them asked.

"Nah, there's just a constable. He can call the state cops if he needs help, but he never does and it would take them forever to get there. They won't come."

"Alright, we'll be there."

Pleased with myself, I turned back toward the ferry just as it was backing away from the landing. *Shit!* I'd missed the boat. I'd be stuck in New London for a couple of hours. I walked up Bank Street to waste some time in the record shop. The store was busy. The owner recognized me and nodded hello.

"How are things out on the island?" he asked. I'm not sure that he knew which island I was from.

"I got a proposition," I said. "There's a beer fest at the lake tomorrow. I'm trying to get people to come. How about if I give you a free pass to give to anyone that buys a record? It'll help sell records."

"I'm closing in a couple hours. You can put a poster in the window if you like."

I bought some poster board and a Magic Marker from the stationery store a couple of doors down. To say that the party was "church-sponsored" was a stretch. But it gave legitimacy to the event. By the time I'd finished, the headline read: *Catholic Church Beer Fest on the Fourth of July.* I hung a poster in the stationer's shop, in the record store window, in the Hygienic Restaurant. I even hung one outside the church downtown. I went into a bar to wait for the ferry.

"What'll you have?"

"Got Pabst?" I asked.

"Are you eighteen?"

"Sure," I said.

He served me on my say-so.

"Whatcha got there?" asked a guy sitting at the bar to my left. He was trying to read the last remaining poster at an angle.

"Beer fest tomorrow," I said. I looked up. He looked older than me. He was wearing a Coast Guard uniform and drinking a Coke.

"Yeah?" He took the poster from me and read it over. "Do you mind if I take this? I know some guys who'd be interested in getting out of New London for a few beers on their day off."

I gave the last poster to the cadet, settled my tab and returned to the ferry terminal to wait for the next boat. The U.S. Mail truck and icehouse delivery truck were waiting in the out-going ferry lines. The mail came every day at this time. The icehouse truck made a trip to the island at least once a day, but almost never this late in the day. The driver and I knew each other by sight.

"How ya doin'?" I asked.

"Oh, man, I'm tired. I'm working too much."

"Yeah, I see you out here every day," I said, sympathetically.

"You see me *twice* a day. I'm on the icehouse truck around noon, but you see me on the milk truck every morning at seven, too. And that's after I've been delivering locally for three hours."

I suddenly realized that I had seen him in the milk truck too. "That's a lot of hours," I said.

"You bet it is. I'm getting loopy. The other day I made double milk deliveries to everyone on the island. I'd made a delivery list of half gallon bottles, but I wrote down 'gallons' instead of 'half gallons.' Then when it was time to load the truck I said to myself: *Gee, that's a lot of milk today.* I didn't even see my own mistake. Everybody who was supposed to get a half gallon got *two* half gallons. When I got back to the dairy, I was nearly fired. I'd cleaned out the walk-in and caused a shortage. I'll never make that mistake again."

"What are you doing out in the ice truck so late in the day?" I asked.

"Someone called in a huge beer and soda order at the last moment. I'm supposed to drop it all at the funeral parlor. That's going to be some funeral!"

"They serve beer at funerals?"

"I guess. There's enough beer in that truck to kill all the mourners—ten half-kegs. I wouldn't have even thought it was possible to find that much beer the day before the Fourth of July, but the caller said 'money is no object.' That's Grolsch, Heineken, Peroni—everything but Pabst. Expensive. My God, I'm tired."

I guessed it was our beer, but being seventeen I didn't want to ask questions that would wise-up any adults to the party.

The ferry arrived. We boarded. The captain sent me back down to help the galley cook for the return trip. The cook gave me a fifteen-minute break as the ferry approached the dock. I stood up on the rail next to a priest.

"It's a lovely place, isn't it?" he said. "Like a picture postcard."

"Yes, Father. Is this your first time here?"

"Yes, it is. I thought I'd see what the island has to offer. I haven't even gotten off the boat, and so far I'm very impressed. I'm Father Francis from New Britain, by the way." He held out his hand.

"It's nice to meet you. My name's Rob. If you need any help—"

"I don't have luggage; I'm just spending a day or so. I could use help getting into town, though—to the Catholic church."

"Evan's the man you want to see. I'll introduce you after we've unloaded the ferry."

Evan and I got off at nine that evening. One of the locals had come over on the ferry with a trunk full of fireworks. Some of it was expensive stuff—multi-stage skyrockets and bricks of M-80s. We blew a few rockets off, but saved the best stuff for the next night, the Fourth of July. It was getting late. I was sitting by a bonfire on the beach with a group of ten kids or so. John Smith, one of Mrs. Smith's sons, had gone home with his younger brother earlier in the evening. But then he appeared again, making his way from the dark end of the beach.

"Hey, Rob," he said discreetly, passing behind me and continuing toward the Crescent Club and home. Allison followed John out of the darkness, twenty steps behind. There were burrs on her sleeve. Her hair was a tousled. She stood next to the fire and said "hey" to the group. She started to sit Indian style in the sand. Evan smoothed out a place beside him and motioned her over. She stood back up and accepted Evan's offer, sitting next to him, opposite the fire from me.

"What were you doing with John?" I asked her through the flames.

Allison looked at me coldly. Evan glared as if to say *don't screw this up for me.*

"Where's the Italian guy?" I taunted her. Evan started looking angry.

"Look, you're just mad because I didn't pick you," she said.

Evan nodded lightly.

"You've picked everybody, from what I can tell," I said.

"Hey! Knock it off," Evan said.

"The problem with you, Rob, is that you're just a baby. I want a real man; a man who is successful, wealthy, and respected in his community—that's the kind of man I want. Someone I could marry someday," she said. None of this described the now-shrinking Evan.

"What's that you want? Cap'n Bob?" I asked, meanly. "Or did you already get him?"

"Fuck you!" Allison stormed off the beach.

"Way to blow it for me, Rob," Evan said.

"I saved your ass," I told him.

{ WILSON }

I was the nighttime maintenance man at the Crescent Club during the summers. It was a good job. I got to leave New London behind for a few months and stay out on the island. Those folks came from a different life than me—I was the only black person on the island. But we got along fine. When they were there, cooking their steaks and having a few drinks, they'd invite me to sit with them. So I did. I was there when people came for a nightcap and a walk on the beach after a hard night of drinking. I saw the beginnings of new romances and scandals—Jack and Liz, Jack and Chloe, Jack and whomever. Couples that shouldn't have been couples, because they were married to other people, didn't hide it from me. They'd ask my advice. I was like the barber or the bartender: they felt comfortable telling their problems to me. Everybody told me everything. Then I kept their darkest secrets, of course. Otherwise they'd have stopped confiding in me.

The other part of my job was running kids off the docks at night, watching out for people who weren't club members, and kicking teenage drinkers out of the parking lot. If you'd summered on the island growing up, then I was part of your childhood; I caught you all making out with each other at fifteen. When you grew up and got married, I chased your kids out of there at night. I'd been doing it for thirty years.

Wednesday night before the Fourth of July was very busy. Folks couldn't wait to blow off their fireworks. There were a lot of people on the beach, a lot of people using the facilities, and a lot of drinking going on. The Crescent Club was a mess. Trashcans were full. Food that had been left out on the picnic tables had been scattered by the seagulls. I made five bucks in forgotten change. I gathered a ball of towels and t-shirts for the lost n' found, which at this point was a regular Salvation Army, with the addition of a forgotten half-bottle of rum. The club finally quieted down around two a.m.

The early morning was humid, and fog set in over the water. I mopped the clubhouse floor, but it wouldn't dry. I opened all the doors and stepped out on the porch for air. I'd already cleaned up out there, but now here were five or so beer cans on a table and a body wrapped in a beach blanket on a wicker couch.

"Who's that?" I demanded of the lumpy blanket.

"Uhh. Oh, hey, Willie."

The lump sat up. A groggy Jack Smith pushed his hair off his forehead and continued: "I was just—"

"You was just keeping away from your wife," I said.

"Yeah—"

"She be crazy. I'd keep away from her too."

He perked up. "Ha! How come you and I are the only ones who know that?"

"Everybody knows it," I said, "but they're all crazy too."

Jack groaned.

"You've been all over the grapevine lately. I heard you been carrying on with Chloe, Liz, Janet and now—Mrs. Steeves' niece. I'm surprised to find you here—a busy man like you. They *all* throw you out?"

"*No!* Mrs. Steeves' niece? Don't say that," Jack pleaded.

"So, you don't deny sleeping with the rest of them."

"I *do* deny it. Especially Janet. Fatty."

"And you was in here drunk the other day. And you're yelling at priests and getting in trouble with the law. You're my hero. Except maybe for the part about beating up old ladies. I'm not sure I feel safe around you," I said.

Jack started laughing.

"And here's the topper," I went on. "The kids are all planning a keg party tomorrow. And they're saying *you're* providing the beer."

"That's news to me," Jack responded. "What kind of beer?"

"I dunno. But it came over on the boat this afternoon—a whole bunch of kegs. Wait 'til Mrs. Garren and Constable Nil get a hold of that. You better hope he gets to you before she does."

Jack frowned. It looked to me like I'd gone on about his troubles a little too long.

"Well, the news isn't *all* about you, anyway," I said. "Father Ivan exploded at the post office today. They said he ripped off his collar and told everyone to fuck themselves."

Jack let out a hearty laugh. "That's fantastic! I wonder if I'm off the hook for the church picnic then."

"Oh they're having the picnic. Though I don't know if the timing is all that good; there's a lot going on at the club tomorrow: breakfast, sailboat races, a white elephant sale."

"White elephant?"

"I guess they couldn't find no black elephants," I said.

Jack chuckled. "Well, I'm going skip out of the picnic early, in any case. I plan to take part in the sailboat races tomorrow. Or today, that is," Jack said.

"Even Father Ivan—or maybe it's just plain old Mr. Ivan now. He's skipping out on the picnic to go racing, too. I bet you get a light crowd up there."

"What's the weather supposed to be?" Jack asked.

"This is it, man. Humid. Maybe a front coming through in the afternoon," I said.

Jack leaned forward and gave each of the cans on the table a gentle shake until he found one that still had a little warm beer in it.

"Sleep medication," he said, throwing it back.

"I hear ya. Well, I gotta do my rounds. Make sure you leave a tip, hear?"

"Yeah. Here's a tip for you: stay away from women."

Thursday, July 4th

I had a lot to do that morning. I shoulda gotten out of there at six-thirty, like I'm supposed to, but club folks started showing up at six to get Fourth of July breakfast underway, and I wasn't going to pass on a plateful of eggs and sausages. Jack beat it out of there at first light.

The Fourth is a day where you see a lot of club members who only come once a year. There's lots of hugging and baby kissing. There's lots of charcoal and burgers. There's khakis, blue blazers, burgees and Top-Siders. By ten a.m., the joint was rocking, the sun was hot, the air was humid, the girls were half-naked, and the beach smelled like coconuts. You had to cross a minefield of transistors blaring Mungo Jerry just to stick your toe in the water. A line formed for breakfast. The flagpole had nautical letter flags draped down both stays, making the Crescent Club look like a used car lot. The little old ladies were setting up for the white elephant sale. I was tired from working third shift, but happy to be part of it all.

The inbound ferries were packed. I couldn't remember having seen that many youngins crushed into muscle cars and family station wagons, ever. They looked like trouble. There weren't any hotels on the island, save for a bed and breakfast. By nine at night, the restaurants would be shut down. Kids would be out on the beaches, late. I knew I'd be hustling the ones that missed the last ferry—throwing them off club property. Constable Nil would be half in the bag and probably have his radio off. If a fight broke out, I would have to let it go. There was only so much I could do. I could understand there being some kids coming over for fireworks and such, but not so early in the day and not so many of them.

I knew that something was up.

{ MRS. STEEVES }

I was in my mid-60s. I'd summered on the island all my life. I met my
husband, Henry, on the island when I was a girl. We were a childless
couple, and kept very much to ourselves. When Henry passed away
unexpectedly, I found myself reaching out to the community around
me and making new friends. I missed Henry dearly, but I was happy
to be part of the community in ways that we never were as a couple.

A few days before the Fourth, Jack Smith, my neighbor across
the way, mistook me for a thief or vandal at his trash barrels. He
knocked me to the ground, crushing me with his great weight.
My shoulder had been giving me problems for some years, and
this exacerbated the pain to a degree where I was sure I'd broken
something. But by the following day, the pain wore off and
disappeared—*completely*. My shoulder felt wonderful. I felt wonderful.
But, I was also left with another sensation. The weight of Jack's body

upon mine had awakened something I hadn't felt since my forties: sexual desire.

Henry and I had enjoyed a narrow sexual pallet over the course of our marriage. I would fantasize of sexual activities that I could never discuss with him. By the time of his death, we rarely had relations, and I believed my lustful yearnings to be behind me. But now, I felt something. I began to notice Jack Smith. I watched his form as he walked away. I studied the corners of his mouth as he spoke. His reputation excited me. Having ample practice suppressing my desires so that I could find Henry's touch sufficient, I knew how to control myself. But now Henry was gone. I could enjoy my fantasies. Jack would never know, but I was enjoying the most lustful *thoughts* of him.

The church picnic was to be the afternoon of the Fourth of July. Father Ivan had nominated me, Loretta Petersen and Jack Smith to organize the event. We had to be ready for the parishioners who would be going up to the lake. Martha Smith, Jack's wife, had volunteered to fill in for Jack in some capacities. Martha and I were loading the wagon. I counted hamburgers, hotdogs, rolls, potato chips, paper plates and napkins.

"Martha, dear," I said. "There are another four or five boxes of hamburgers out back. I didn't have room in the kitchen refrigerator."

Martha went to look for the hamburgers.

Oh, I mustn't forget the pie, I thought. The pie was for the winners of the Fourth of July decorating contest—a couple from the other end of the bay. They were to stop by for the award at the picnic. Martha hadn't won the contest and I didn't want to address the awful mess she'd made of her porch—at this point a collection of matted brushes and spilled paints. While she was busy in the storage shed, I quietly tucked the plastic-wrapped pie into a bag and stowed it below the back seat of the car, out of sight.

"Allison, dear, would you look in the back closet for a red and white checkered tablecloth?" I was hoping to put my niece, Allison, to some good use. Earlier in the morning, she'd shown no interest in helping with preparations or in attending the picnic at all. She changed her mind quite suddenly, owing to what I do not know. Allison was a good girl, though a little capricious. She was precocious, too. Her parents had fetched her from some unmentionable situations and she'd been seeing a psychiatrist. I was to keep an eye on her through her summer visit, though this day we would have plenty of adults around, so the burden would be somewhat diluted.

"Oh, there you are, Martha. Did you have trouble finding the hamburgers?"

"No problem," she replied. The fresh smell of alcohol on her breath attested to the delay in the pantry. I let it go. *Poor Jack*, I thought. Perhaps he'd had a difficult time living with Martha. I pictured the two of them together. Then I imagined me wandering off with Jack at the picnic, leaving her behind.

Allison returned with a sad-looking crushed plastic tablecloth. It had musty cotton backing that smelled like an old tent. I was going to suggest she toss the tablecloth out, but instead directed her to pack it into a bag. Martha held the bag open.

"How old are you now, Allison?" Martha asked.

"Sixteen."

"Oh, come on now," I interjected. "You won't be sixteen until Thanksgiving time." She was always exaggerating her age and getting into trouble for it.

"I think that's it," said Martha, shutting the rear hatch of the car.

"Now, you're sure that someone will be delivering soft drinks?" I asked.

"All set," Martha assured me.

Allison and I slid into the station wagon. Martha begged out, saying that she had to attend to her children. She assured us she'd see us at the picnic. Allison and I followed the road that leads away from the shore up to the island dump, power plant, water supply and freshwater lake.

The island lake was a lovely spot. There were oaks, maples and pines. You wouldn't know that you were so close to the sea by the look of it, except for the smell of the salty air. From one particular spot, you could see almost all the way around the island. This day was humid and hazy. As we came up the hill, I spied the ferry coming in, sailboats, American flags and party tents. It was a beautiful summer day.

When we approached the picnic grounds it became apparent that we weren't the only group present. I saw few cars I recognized and many that I didn't know at all. They were parked about the perimeter of the lot, outside the designated lines. Untold numbers of teenagers sat on their hoods and trunks. More crisscrossed the lot in the hot sun—most holding beverages. Music blared from several open vehicles. One youngster drove his loud, shiny vehicle spinning in a circle with smoking tires. *Doing doughnuts*, my niece informed me.

I parked timidly and out of the way. I pulled my pie from under the seat. We walked up the incline with a couple of bags to the area where the grills were located. I offered indignant words to an amorous young pair groping one another on a picnic table: "Now see here! This is a church picnic!"

Jack Smith's car entered the lot. He stepped out and looked around at the pandemonium. From within the gang of teenagers, Evan, a dockhand for the ferry, approached Jack and shook his hand. Evan looked out among the crowd, called some names and waved a dozen or so teenagers over to him. They followed in a loose pack up the last stretch of the hill from the parking area to where we stood by the grills. Jack arrived several steps ahead of them.

"Hi, Agnes. How's the shoulder?" Jack asked.

"I'm fine. Thank you, Jack. All is forgiven," I said, giving him a hug. "You've met my niece?"

Jack turned to Allison. "Oh yes, of course we've met," he said, nodding to her, cordially.

That was the end of the small talk. The scene before us was a teenage zoo. I suspected that a number of people would choose to remain at the beach on a summer day like this, anyway. But it looked as though, with the exception of the rabble-rousers, there were no churchgoers at all. We learned that Loretta Peterson had arrived sometime earlier with the makings of games: potato sacks, spoons, eggs and beanbags. These appeared to have become fodder for mischief with the teenagers.

Evan and his small band of youths stepped up. Allison found a place in the shadows as they approached. Evan introduced his ragtag group of friends to us as the cooks and helpers for the picnic. I was a little taken aback. This crowd had appeared as though they'd usurped the facility and ruined the occasion. Now, there was a detachment of them volunteering.

"Well, okay," I said, thinking that the situation might be righting itself after all. I directed them back down to the parking lot to unload my station wagon. As they made their way, a hearse pulled in and Mrs. Puljcisz' son stepped out. A few of the boys went over to greet him. Many more came to inspect the hearse. He swung open the doors in the rear of the vehicle and loaded the boys' arms with bags of ice and cases of soda. As he opened a side door, a cheer rang out from the crowd. Groups of teenagers in threes and fours carried beer kegs from the open hearse over the shady area on the far side of the lot.

"When is Father Ivan going to be here?" I demanded to no one. "And where is Constable Howard? This looks like trouble!"

I began walking down the hill to have a word with Mrs. Puljcisz' boy, but he stepped back into the hearse and departed before I could reach him. I am *certain* I saw Martha Smith in the passenger's seat. Exasperated, I returned to the picnic area. Several automobiles belonging to church members entered the parking lot, surveyed the hoopla and left. Once the hearse had discharged its contents, the success of the picnic was in grave danger.

"I'm going to look for Father Ivan. Come along, Allison."

"Can't I stay here?" she whined.

I gave the request a moment's thought. Typically, I'd have demanded that she come with me, given her penchant for mischief, but I thought I might have some unsavory business to conduct. I turned to Jack Smith: "Will you look after my grand-niece?" I continued on in hushed tones: "Please keep an eye on her. She tends toward poor judgment when left on her own." I trusted Jack completely.

{ ALLISON }

Jack and I watched my craggy old aunt leave.

"Look at all the red ants," he said, looking for something to say.

I inspected my aunt's pie, to see that it was wrapped well enough so that the ants couldn't get to it.

"Do you want a beer?" I asked.

"I do. But *you* can't be drinking beer. Your aunt would kill me."

"Oh, I'm not going to drink any. I'm not allowed to," I said.

Jack shot me a glance. "I thought you were eighteen," he said.

"I mean, I'm old enough—I'm almost nineteen, but my aunt doesn't think I should drink."

Jack bit his lip and thought it over.

"I'll get you one," I said. I jumped off the picnic table and ran down the path to the parking lot before there could be any more discussion.

I returned a few moments later with two beers in plastic cups.

"I thought you said you weren't going to drink any."

"I can have *one*."

The beer tasted good. Jack and I sat next to one another on the top of a picnic table far enough removed from the other tables to be anyone's last choice. Jack knocked back his beer.

"Want another?"

"One more," he said.

I came back with two more. I sat back down next to him and began rubbing his back.

"Hey! Someone will see you."

"I don't care."

"Well, I do," he insisted.

I turned and looked into his eyes, dangerously close to kissing him. He closed his eyes, took a deep breath and leaned toward me. His hand knocked the beer off the table as he moved it to brace himself in the new position.

"Yikes!" I said, jumping off the table, laughing. My pants were soaked.

"I'm so sorry!" he said. I loved the way he looked at me—so apologetic and sweet. I rocked up on my tiptoes and kissed him as he fumbled for words.

"I'll get you another," I whispered. I ran down to the parking lot.

What a magical summer it was turning out to be. I'd been to the island with my parents as a little kid, but it was never this much fun. The beach, the nights, the boys.

My old aunt slept pretty soundly. I could sneak out and do what I wanted at night. She couldn't even tell when I was stoned or drunk.

My parents sent me to spend the summer with Aunt Agnes because they didn't like my friends. I'd been caught with a little pot and suspended a couple of times for some other stuff. They made me see this creepy psychiatrist and I had to report to a juvenile detention officer. They watched me like hawks. If my parents only knew the fun I was having on the island—they'd have flipped.

I came back up the hill from the parking lot, carefully carrying two beers and a plastic cup half-full of rum, plus a few extra cups for shots.

"Where'd that come from?" Jack asked, nodding at the rum.

"Mike, I think was his name. He's one of the stewards. Want a shot?"

"One," Jack said, though there was enough rum in the plastic cup for two, each. The parking lot was packed at that point. Car radios were turned up loudly to competing stations, so that it all became noise. The boys were serving up church-picnic burgers. The sky was getting heavy and dark, as though we might get a thunderstorm. I was drunk.

"Fuck my parents!" I raised a toast to the whole scene. "I'll get you another beer."

"No, no, no!" he said. "I gotta pee."

I went for more beer, but when I returned Jack wasn't at the table. I walked into the woods in the direction I'd guessed he'd gone, dragging the plastic tablecloth behind me. I met him on the path. We were far enough away from the parking lot that the blaring music was tolerable.

"Do you want to go sit on that rock?" I asked.

"Sure." He took the next beer from my hand.

We chatted, flicking an occasional red ant. I watched the corners of his mouth as he spoke. I reach up to touch one of the corners with my finger. He stopped speaking and leaned into me for a gentle kiss. We kissed, and then kissed again, passionately, hungrily. Jack spread the tablecloth over the ground behind the rock and lifted me down.

"We should stop. Jesus, this is wrong." He screwed up his face as he smelled his fingers—the smell of the musty tablecloth.

"It's not wrong if it feels good. And it feels good to me," I said, kissing him softly on the neck.

He thought about it. He openly mulled over this being a picnic sponsored by the church. He stuck his head up several times and looked around. He told me he had the best intentions. He was also very nervous about being discovered—even more so than before.

"Let them find us," I sang out. "I'll happily tell the world. I'm in love with Jack Smith!"

"Don't say that," he hissed. He straightened himself out and began pacing the area.

I shrugged my shoulders, smiled and let out a little chuckle.

"I have to pee again," he said, nervously.

"Me too. See you in five."

The sky looked like it was about to rain. I walked in one direction, toward the outhouses. Jack headed in the other, toward the trees. I peaked over my shoulder to watch him walk as he disappeared into the woods. As I turned back to the path, from behind me there came a flash and crack of thunder so loud and so sharp that it knocked me down. Rain started instantly. Torrents! The kids in the parking lot scrambled for cars and the covered picnic areas. Steam billowed from the grills. Soaking wet, I turned to see where Jack had gone. I had been so happy. Suddenly, I was worried that he might be hurt.

{ JACK'S FIRST NEAR-DEATH EXPERIENCE }

Jack surveyed a space that had no discernible walls, just fading blackness. He sat on a hassock of mist. Above him was the sky and trees, partially obscured by his lightning-scored body, still smoking in the pouring rain. Nickel-sized raindrops fell and danced about his dead form, viewed from below as though through a sheet of foggy Plexiglas.

Lilly sat across from him. Only this wasn't a confused, muttering Lilly. This was an omniscient, luminous Lilly, though she was old and haggard just the same. Her eyes focused on him, waiting for his first words:

"What is this?" Jack asked.

"You're dead," Lilly answered.

"But—," Jack began.

Lilly cut him off. "Do you know that girl is only fifteen?"

"She said she was almost nineteen!"

"Eh, who cares how old she is, really."

"I don't feel that way about it."

"Really? Now that you're dead, you may as well be honest. It won't make you any deader."

"What about judgment?"

"Judgment? By whom? In the end, the universe and everything anyone ever knew about it gets consumed in flames. It's like nothing ever happened, and nobody keeps score," Lilly said.

Jack was quiet for a moment, and then returned to the subject of himself: "*Dead?* Why am I here talking to you then? This isn't heaven..."

"No. There's no heaven. When you're dead, that's it. You had a beach house. What more did you want? Why dismiss the whole journey of life in expectation of something better? It's pretty selfish, if you ask me."

"I don't understand, then. If there's nothing else, then what am I doing here?"

"Consider this a *near-death* experience. You're as dead as you can get, except that your brain's still got a few minutes before it turns to mush."

"But, I don't want to die."

"Alright," Lilly said. "I'm agreeable to that. There's more you can do."

"You mean, I can go back?"

"Sure, I'll send you back. But, live a better life. Stay away from that girl. Or—not. You thought I should give advice like that, so I did. Really, I can't threaten you with retribution. Heck, do whatever you like. I'm not even sure that I'm not part of your imagination. Do me a favor. When you're back there, kill my extant self, would you? She's half dead as it is. If you hit her with a pick axe I might be able to leave this fucking place."

{ ALLISON, AGAIN }

I found Jack lying on his back, propped up on his elbows. The rain had stopped and the sun was peeking out. Like everything around him, Jack was soaking wet.

"So much for angels," he muttered.

"What? Let me help you up."

I put an arm around Jack's shoulder and tugged him to his feet. He fixed on me as if I were his mother.

"I just love you," he said.

"Were you hit by lightning?" I asked. He had been as nervous as a Chihuahua a few minutes earlier. Now he acted almost drugged. I was afraid he might be injured.

"So what if you're only fifteen?" he said.

"Who told you that?" I looked around, wondering who could've ratted on me.

Jack got to his feet and started to walk—shaky and stumbling at first, and then better.

"I'm starving," he said.

We reached the grills. They smelled like wet charcoal. The leftover rolls were soaked through. The hamburgers and hotdogs had been charred on the grill and then doused by rain.

"The pie!" Jack gasped, noticing my aunt's pie on a bench, still sealed. He ripped the bag apart like a hungry bear. He dug into the pie with his fingers, threw back his head and forced a wedge into his mouth. No sooner had he swallowed the first bite than he began choking and pounding his chest.

"Jesus!" he exclaimed. He rubbed the heel of his hand up and down his sternum and arched his back, contorting to make something pass. "I swallowed a pit."

"That's a strawberry pie," I said. "There are no pits."

He rubbed a flattened palm over his stomach. His face had a sour expression.

"What the hell was it?"

He continued writhing to make whatever he swallowed find a resting place. The breeze in the trees eventually took his attention away from his gut.

"The race," he said.

"What?" I asked.

"Sailboat race. I have to go."

"Take me."

"Sure," he said, "Why not? You know, some people say that in the end, the universe and everything anyone ever knew about it gets consumed in flames. It's like nothing ever happened, and nobody keeps score."

"Far out! That's just how I feel about it," I said.

We trotted down to the parking lot and into the warm sunshine. The party had started up again and grown much larger and louder. A small cheer went up for Jack when the crowd saw us. Jack raised a triumphant fist and edged his car gently through the throng of teenagers, out of the lake area and down the central road to the shore. My aunt's wagon approached us from the other direction at high speed. Father Ivan was in the passenger's seat, pressed against the windshield as if to reach the picnic area sooner. The constable was driving. My aunt was in the back seat. I ducked down as they passed, then jumped up, turned around and flipped them the bird.

"Fuck you, Aunty Agony!" I shouted.

Jack laughed. "Cigarette?" He'd found an old pack of Martha's in the car.

"Sure," I said, taking one.

We stepped from the car in the overflow parking lot at the Crescent Club. It had become a bright, beautiful day. There was a breeze to replace the morning's humidity. Flags were flying. The beach was packed. The club was alive with activity. Jack took a draw on his cigarette.

"It's good to be alive," Jack said, coughing.

It was great to be alive! This was already the best day of my summer. I could imagine it being the best day of my life. I threw myself into Jack's arms and kissed him passionately in the parking lot, out in the open, and then walked hand-in-hand with him toward the club.

{ CAP'N BOB }

It was the race committee's job to set up the sailing course, conduct the races and record the results. In most of our races, we had three components: a starting line, a windward mark and a leeward mark. Typically, the sailboats first competed to reach the windward mark. As boats arrived at the windward mark, they would round it and race toward the leeward mark. Upon reaching that, they returned to the starting line to finish the race. When we had multiple races, as we often did, the placements were averaged to reach a final score for each boat. It all happened on the water. Seamanship and technique mattered. And I kept score.

The racing marks were inflatable buoys. They had light anchors so that we could place them or move them wherever we choose. As the wind might be different from one day to the next, the placement of the marks would change too. Our most important consideration for setting up the course was to place the marks so that the leeward mark was directly downwind of the windward mark. This made for the most competitive racing. A boat cannot sail directly into the wind, so it had to *beat* a zigzag path to a windward mark. If the marks were aligned, it meant that neither side of the course would be favored; zigs would be as good as zags.

The starting line was formed by a gap between a boat—the race committee boat—and a smaller inflatable buoy, called the *pin*. The starting line was perpendicular to and centered upon an imaginary line from the windward mark to the leeward mark. The competitors gathered just downwind of the starting line at the start of a race. The race committee started the race on a clock—three minutes, two minutes, one minute and thirty, one minute, thirty seconds, twenty seconds, ten seconds, five, four, three, two, one, go!

The starting line could be very hectic. Boats were almost always under weigh, sailing fast and crossing one another. At the final moments leading up to a start, boats would compete for position on the line. Their sails were hauled in. The boats were healing and close together. The crews' total concentrations would be on making the boat fast and on making a good start. Such is the concentration that a captain wouldn't expect an encounter with a non-racing boat sailing equally fast, just on the wrong side of the starting line, as would happen on this day.

The weather had cleared and a prevailing southwesterly took over at about eight knots. Seated at a picnic table beneath the Crescent Club tent, I demonstrated knot-tying to a few lads I'd snagged.

"The rabbit goes around the tree, through the hole," I repeated. They invariably tied grannies. I soon lost them to the ice cream truck.

In the sunshine, near the clubhouse entrance, the club manager handled requests and directed his stewards on this busy day, though watching his face and looking around for myself I gathered that the stewards weren't anywhere to be found. I stood, steadied myself, and walked stiffly over to inquire about my helpers on the race committee, and to see whether the committee boat was ready and whether the marks were inflated.

"I can't find them," exclaimed Tommy, the club manager,

referring to his stewards. "They've been missing since about eleven."

It was just after one o'clock. The course had to be set and the starting line had to be readied. The race would begin at two. Although reluctant to leave his post, Tommy agreed to fill in for the missing stewards and help me set the course.

The Crescent Club had two small Boston whalers and a skiff. One whaler served as the race committee platform. The other would be the mark boat for setting marks and observing the sailors as they rounded the buoys. The skiff, less seaworthy, would stay behind to ferry club members out of their moorings. With no stewards to pilot the skiff, Tommy enlisted the night caretaker, Wilson, who had been dozing on the porch for some hours.

As Tommy and I discussed our plan of action, Jack Smith stepped up with a young girl in tow. They were soon joined by Lawrence Puljcisz, the undertaker, who stepped out of the clubhouse to meet them. Lawrence had a bag of sails over his shoulder. Jack asked Tommy for a lift to his boat and Tommy deferred Jack to Wilson.

Wilson slumped sweating in a chair, wiping the sleep out of his eyes. Within a minute or so, a small crowd had gathered around him. Every third person carried a sail bag. Wilson reluctantly embraced the assignment.

"Which boat is yours?" Wilson asked each team of sailors who encircled him. He tried to organize them to make the minimum number of excursions to the mooring field.

"Who's got the grey boat?" he asked. Nobody volunteered. By the time he'd ferried everyone to their boats, only the nearly sunken grey boat was without a crew.

Tommy and I departed the club dock, each piloting our own Boston whaler. We set up the windward and leeward marks and trued the starting line in a light southwest breeze. It went easily; we were ready in time for the two o'clock start. If a boat is late to the starting line, then it's late to the race. There are no exceptions.

Zip-class boats approached the starting area and sailed all about us. Nineteen boats—more than had ever sailed a single race at the Crescent Club. At a ten 'til two, we saw the twentieth Zip—the grey one—leave the moorings en route to the starting line. She'd likely be late. At two o'clock, precisely, we blew a gathering horn and started the race sequence.

Three long horn blasts signaled three minutes. Zips sailed parallel to the starting line, one end to the other, just missing one another in a ballet governed by sailing right-of-way rules. The breeze began to stiffen and the boats moved faster. The grey boat continued to make her way to the starting area.

Honk, honk! Tommy blew the starting horn twice; two minutes to go. The wind picked up to twelve knots or so. An occasional wave crest broke.

Honk, honk-honk-honk! One minute, thirty seconds. Out of nowhere, the wind built to over twenty knots. White caps were prevalent. The boats darted up and down the line at hull speed, healing and bucking in the wind shadows of their competitors. Suddenly, the line seemed a bit short for this many boats and this much wind. The grey boat neared. I thought she might make it in time.

Honk! Tommy blew the one-minute warning. I wondered about the whereabouts of my brother, Ivan. I should have seen him by now. Technically, each boat has to check in with the race committee, but he hadn't done so. Then, all at once, I could see who was piloting the grey boat. It was Ivan. Constable Nil was hiked out to hold the boat level. But this was not Ivan's boat; Ivan's boat was red, white and blue. I wasn't certain whose boat it was. I couldn't imagine why they were aboard her.

Honk-honk-honk! Thirty seconds. With this much wind, the battleship grey Zip was going to make it just it in time for the start of the race; Ivan and Nil would be the twentieth boat. This was exciting, even if a bit confusing!

Honk-Honk! Twenty seconds. There she was, bearing down on the starting line.

Honk! Ten seconds. Competitors were tacking and jibing in the heavy breeze. Some spilled wind from their sails in preparation for the final stab at the line. The grey boat was just a matter of yards from the committee boat and the starting line.

I could see Ivan and Nil's faces clearly. They showed no joy at all.

Honk! Five seconds. They were close.

Honk! Four seconds. They were going to make it just in time for the start.

Honk! Three seconds. They veered. *Where were they going?* They were heading for the wrong side of the committee boat—the wrong side of the starting line.

Honk! Two seconds. They were going to pass in *front* of the committee boat. That's not allowed.

Honk! One second. Ivan and Nil sailed right past the committee boat on a beam reach, moving very quickly into the emerging fleet of starting boats.

BOOM! Tommy shot the starting gun. It was followed by a loud crack, snapping, banging and shouting. The grey boat broadsided Jack Smith's boat so forcefully that the topside planks of Jack's boat sprung and the boat foundered. Jack Smith, Lawrence Puljcisz and constable Nil Howard were thrown into the water with the impact. The other boats in the area fouled one another in a series of collisions I'd never seen the likes of. Ivan jumped from the grey boat into the froth, reaching Jack in an instant.

"I'll baptize *you!*" he shouted.

The girl remained on the sinking boat, clinging to the mast, looking too frightened to cry for help. Nil and Ivan ganged up on Jack, pushing his head underwater for an extended time. Nil grasped Jack around the neck while Ivan punched wildly at his head and torso. Lawrence, the undertaker, swam to Jack's aid. The water churned with malevolence and intercession.

A second wave of swimmers went into the water to break up the melee. Eventually, they pulled the priest and the policeman off Jack. A fleet of damaged boats, some with broken masts, bumped, rubbed and bucked in the angry seas. The gaps between boats opened and closed in the pounding waves, in a few cases forcing sailors to swim out from underneath their boats in order to escape. Jack was lost for a time when such a gap closed. The flapping sails made all vocal communication impossible; each person was left to their own sense of right. Eventually, the churning group pushed and tugged Jack toward the race committee boat. The undertaker and a couple of helpful souls pushed him into the whaler and I sped back to the club with him. Jack's unconscious, bruised form lay on the floor of the boat. His head absorbed the pounding insult of each wave we crossed.

Reaching the dock, I signaled to the onlookers that I had an emergency on my hands—that I was trying to tug a person from the whaler. Eventually, six or seven women rushed down and carried Jack off like pallbearers and set him on a chaise lounge on the porch. The rest of the membership gathered to take in the excitement. When I'd finally pushed my way through the throng, I found a suffocatingly tight group of do-gooders crowding the unconscious Jack.

One woman, who would later admit she was just trying to help but didn't really know what she was doing, pushed down repeatedly on Jack's stomach as though he were a drowned cartoon character on the verge of producing a fish. Instead, he vomited in a forceful arc. The encircling assembly, who had at first bent forward at the waist over Jack like the petals of a closed flower, now arched backward, hyper-extended like the tatters of an exploded cigar. Baptized in bile, seawater, and beer, the only person who hazarded the trajectory a second time was Jack's wife, Martha. She extended the toe of her shoe into the vomitus, drew a curio back to her person, plucked it up, wiped it down and stowed it in her pocket. One of the clubmember's guests, a bona fide medical professional, now attended to Jack Smith.

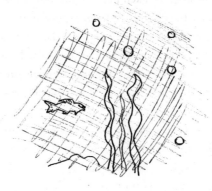

{ JACK'S SECOND NEAR-DEATH EXPERIENCE }

Once again, Jack was seated in the fading blackness. He viewed the scene of his pending death from below. Gathered around his prostrate form were Maura Garren, Elizabeth, Chloe, Martha, Agnes Steeves, Laurie, Loretta Peterson, Janet—all of them. Each deeply concerned for their own reasons.

"It's quite moving, really," Jack said, turning to Lilly. "I didn't know they loved me so much."

"They're insane," she replied. "Survive this, and you're going to owe each of them a life of servitude. Die, and it's *Jack was so nice* and *I miss Jack so much*. You're probably better off dead."

Jack frowned at Lilly. "What's your problem, anyway? Aren't you here to help me? A near-death experience is supposed to be beautiful and, just like last time, you're bitter. You're ruining this for me."

Just then, Jack noticed Janet trying to resuscitate his drowned body by pushing on its belly. "Whoa!" he barked when the vomit ejected from his unconscious form. A regurgitated key landed just above his head with a ping. He could make out *USPS* clearly.

"The pit from the pie!" he exclaimed.

Jack watched Martha kick the key from the bile. He began to protest and then chuckled: "I want her to have that, actually."

"Maybe not," Lilly said. "There's a note from Katrin in the post office box. She wants to come back for her bicycle, she writes, but the real reason for the letter is that she wants to see you."

Jack was quiet for a moment and then looked over the crowd of women tending lovingly to his bluing form.

"To hell with Katrin," he said.

"That's the smartest thing you've said all day," Lilly replied.

Jack surveyed the goings-on over his head. Real medical help arrived. One of the women covered his body with a blanket. It affected him. He bit his lower lip. He asked: "How could I could be a pariah one moment and the club darling the next? These people are treating me like they actually care about me."

Lilly didn't respond.

Jack began to worry about the passing minutes and whether he was going to recover. "I survive this, right?"

"I don't know. Do you want to?"

"You mean I might not?"

"They extended your time by trying to revive you, but your brain's going to die soon. I think that means your near-death experience will come to an end, too. I think that'll be the end of me as well. In fact, in your universe, we all may cease to exist if you're not here to experience us."

"You told me nothing matters. It all ends in fire. A waste of time, right?"

Lilly nodded. Just then, Jack's boys rushed into the picture, wide-eyed and horrified at the sight of someone performing mouth-to-mouth resuscitation on his unconscious body. A couple of the old hens ushered the boys away. Without another moment's delay Jack exclaimed: "Send me back!"

"What makes you think I can do that?" Lilly asked.

"I could be brain-dead by now. Hurry!"

"I don't know how."

"What? How will I get back?"

"I'm just jiving you," Lilly said. "Here you go."

{ CAP'N BOB, AGAIN }

Jack came to life. He sat up. In fact, it was more spectacular than that: he smiled. This was a man who, moments before, was suffering asphyxia and could be looking forward to considerable complications from water in the lungs, if he were to survive at all.

"There's no place like home," were his first words to the doctor and me. He pushed off the chaise lounge and began coughing deeply.

"Where do you think you're going?" the doctor asked. "You nearly drowned."

"I've got to look out for the wellbeing of the boys." He stumbled out into the sunshine with the crowd surrounding the tent. A cheer broke out as if Lazarus walked among them.

By now, the remnants of the wounded fleet had sailed back or were towed in, piece-by-piece. The sodden figures of Ivan and Nil were escorted up the dock by the other sailors like ironed malefactors. Their eyes followed the commotion up to the tent, and at the sight of a vivacious Jack, they fell to their knees, their burdens lifted. The girl ran past them, up the dock to the where the crowd gathered. She jumped onto Jack like a cat to a post, hugging him and kissing his neck. Lawrence the undertaker, robbed of a bit of business, followed more slowly, but beaming all the same.

"I'm fine," Jack assured everyone, coughing. "I've never felt better in my life."

The toll to the fleet would be counted another day. Ivan and Nil wandered off the premises, free to go for the time being. Jack was king that day. He made a throne of a wicker chair on the Crescent Club porch. Martha tended to him, patiently accepting the presence of other women, and they her. The club bar opened early and the wine, beer and liquor flowed until evening. The nighttime sky would be alight with fireworks—sanctioned and otherwise. A preponderance of drunken off-islanders—mostly teenagers—would celebrate along with us, pushing the envelope of good behavior, but generally on the side of decency. They would evoke the name of Jack Smith as their hero. At dawn, the beach would be littered with gnat-eaten revelers, snoring in the sand in their soggy clothes.

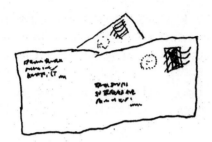

{ DONNA GRIMALDI }

My name is Donna Grimaldi. My son, Nicky, was friends with the Smith boys. My daughter Patty and I had been over to the Smith house to pick flowers earlier in the week, and Martha had come back to our house for dinner.

It was the afternoon of the Fourth of July, and I was searching for Patty at the Crescent Club. The other girls in her age group hadn't seen her for a while. The church picnic had turned into another Woodstock, and there was so much drunkenness and so many strangers on the island that I became anxious.

"Patty?" I called out on the beach. "Has anyone seen my daughter Patty?" I looked in the craggy beach spots where kids wade and crab. "Have you seen Patty?"

"She *was* here," one little boy told me. "She went with a lady."

"A lady? Do you know who?"

He shook his head *no*. I stood tall and scanned the water, beaches, docks, clubhouse tent for a lady with a child. There were many.

"Do you know where they went?"

"Mmm-mmm." He shook his head *no* again.

My next thought was to look for the constable. I sighed when I recalled what had become of him that afternoon. The whole world seemed turned upside down. I would have valued my husband John's help, but I didn't want to go all the way back to the cottage to get him. Having exhausted a foot-search for Patty around the ferry dock and Crescent Club, I backed the car from the club lot and headed up the beach road.

Thank God! There was Patty, walking along the beach, alone. I stopped and waved her over. She ran up the beach to the car. She carried something in her hands.

"Where have you been? I was worried sick about you!"

"I was—"

"What's that in your hand?"

Patty silently handed over what she was holding—someone's mail.

"What's this?" I asked.

"I'm not supposed to say."

"Not supposed to say?"

I looked over the small bundle of mail. It was all addressed to Jack Smith. There was a postcard.

> *Dear Jack,*
> *I am coming to the island Saturday, 6 July. I hope that is okay for you. I wish to have my bicycle and I hope that we can talk. I need you to understand that I did not leave because of the money. Bis Samstag.*
> *Katrin*

"Why do you have this?" I asked Patty.

"It's a secret." Patty diverted her eyes.

"A secret? It's time to tell me your secret, young lady."

"Well—" she looked distraught. "Mrs. Smith gave me five dollars to get the mail and told me not to tell anyone, especially you."

There was also an envelope from Dennis Burke, a banker. The flap was barely glued shut. I ran my finger underneath and pulled out a hand-written letter.

> *Dear Mrs. Smith,*
>
> *I just got off the phone with your husband. I am aware that you are intercepting his mail. I personally find that deplorable. Moreover, I am saddened that he would, in turn, ask me to craft a falsified letter for you to read.*
>
> *I am hereby formally resigning as your banker. I will graciously transfer your accounts wherever you choose. For your own good, you should plan to come home and deal with your debts.*
>
> *Dennis Burke*
>
> *P.S.: In case Jack hasn't told you, he is bankrupt. The only protected piece of property, the beach house, is in your name and you are the sole insurance beneficiary.*

In spite of my denials to Martha Smith, I'd known Katrin. I thought she was sweet. But she and Jack had made a conspicuous pair, being so far apart in years. Katrin seemed sincerely interested in Jack, but everyone assumed she was also in interested in his money. She'd clearly discovered that Jack was broke before Martha had.

I was upset that Martha had dragged my little Patty into her marital mischief. I decided that I would dispatch the letters myself. And if I was going to be the bearer of bad news, then I would take some vengeance from it.

Patty leaned in the driver's side window. "Go back to the Crescent Club and stay with your friends. I am going to visit the Smiths." She read the resolution in my face and obediently continued down the beach.

I found Jack and Martha on their porch, sharing a loveseat rocker. Martha smoked a cigarette and drank from a glass of scotch. Jack sat empty-handed. As I approached, Martha set her glass down and put an arm around Jack's shoulders.

"Good afternoon, Donna," Martha said.

"Some day! Full of surprises," I replied.

"I'm lucky to be alive," Jack said.

"Did you hear about Jack's incident?" Martha asked.

"Yes, everybody knows everything. Or they will pretty soon, anyway."

"Tell Donna how you feel, Jack," Martha directed.

"I'm so happy to have another chance with my family," Jack said. Yet, his facial expression said, *Get me out of here.*

"I have your mail," I said.

Martha's face went white.

"This is a postcard from Katrin," I said, handing Jack the card. "And this is a letter addressed to Jack from your banker. You were supposed to intercept this, weren't you Martha? Isn't that why you hired my daughter to empty Jack's mail box?" I handed her the letter. "She's no longer working for you."

Jack and Martha sat frozen, each with an incriminating piece of mail in hand. It was apparent that neither would dare read their letters with the other nearby, so I paraphrased for both of them:

"Jack, Katrin is coming on Saturday. She wants her bicycle. I think she also wants to assuage her conscience. That should be a nice discussion. It certainly won't be a chat about money. She made that clear in the note. Martha will get to meet her at long last."

Jack stared into the floor. Martha's brow furrowed.

"Martha, the letter from the banker says that Jack is broke. Furthermore, the banker says he quits. The banker sounds an awful lot like Katrin, don't you think?"

Neither said anything. It was frustrating for me; I wanted fireworks.

"But there's some good news, Martha," I continued. "Apparently, you own this house."

Martha's eyes widened. She looked around the porch, at the ceilings, columns and floor—her new possessions. "The floor could use a coat of grey paint," she said.

"Did you hear anything I said?" I demanded.

Martha took a drag from her cigarette and resumed pushing the rocker. "We nearly lost Jack today, you know. He and I can rise above any tragedy. We've discovered that a family has to stick together. Isn't that right, Jack?"

Jack looked up at me in desperation.

"Don't ever speak to my daughter again," I demanded and left.

{ JOHN SMITH }

My brother Mark and I sat on the beach with Rob, one of the dockhands for the ferry and some of his friends. The whole world smelled like gunpowder. The main fireworks display was over, but there were plenty of others going off all around us. We could see tons of fireworks over on the Connecticut side too.

There were groups of older kids on the beach. Some of them were a little wild and scary. Most of them weren't from here. There were bonfires. The Crescent Club was lit up. The last ferry had left. There was no supervision. It was exciting, but Mark and I looked to Rob for protection, too.

"Want some, John?" Rob asked, offering a bottle.

"Sure," I said.

"John! Mom'll kill you!" Mark interrupted.

"Only if you tell her. And if you do, I'll kill *you*," I scolded him.

I took a swig and held back the need to cough. I handed the

bottle back to Rob.

"Pretty good," I said.

Mark looked away.

"Your dad's the big hero around here, you know," said Rob.

"Yeah," I said, though I wasn't really sure why dad qualified as a hero for nearly getting killed.

"That priest is crazy," Rob continued. "He flipped out in the post office the other day, and then he tried to drown your dad. We always knew there was something wrong with him." The other fellows nodded in agreement. "Besides," Rob went on, "your dad threw us a huge party at the lake today."

"Yeah, but why did Father Ivan and Constable Howard try to kill my dad?" I asked. I knew that my dad hadn't exactly been the most popular man in town. I'd heard people call him a drunkard and a skirt-chaser. Suddenly he was a hero, and I couldn't see what had actually changed.

An M-80 went off down the beach. It was *so* loud; it seemed to suck up all the sound around it the instant before it exploded. Mark looked nervous.

"I'm ready to go home now," Mark whined.

"Hang in there for a few more minutes," I prodded him. I knew that when he left, I'd have to go with him. I continued my thought: "Was it because my dad took Father Ivan's boat?"

"Yeah. That pissed off the priest," said Rob. "Royally."

"But he didn't know it wasn't his."

"That's no reason to try to kill someone," Evan chimed in.

"Plus, your dad bought all the beer," said Rob. "It turned the church picnic into a total keg party."

BOOM! Another M-80.

"Can we go, please?" implored Mark.

"Hang on," I said, and reached out to Rob for the bottle one more time. I took a final swig.

"Alright," I said. "Let's go."

Mark was up in an instant and already a few anxious steps on his way. I brushed the sand off my pants and was making my goodbyes to the group. There was another boom—this time from a different direction. It was much duller and farther off than the M-80s. The noise was followed by the sound of lumber and falling debris.

"Oh, no!" Mark cried out.

"What's wrong," I asked.

Mark pointed up the road. "That's our house!"

"No, it's not." It couldn't be. But the group looked up the hill to see smoke and fire where our house should have been.

"Let's go!" I shouted.

We all ran by the Crescent Club and up the hill to the fire.

{ JACK'S THIRD NEAR-DEATH EXPERIENCE }

Jack was in the fading darkness for the third time that day. This time he was naked.

"What the hell was that?" he asked. Above him he saw fire and smoke. There were legions of scurrying black and red ants. He could see Janet's family gathered near the conflagration, as if it were for their amusement. Among them was the doddering, real-world Lilly, eating a raw hot dog without a bun.

"Oops," said near-death-experience Lilly. "That wasn't supposed to happen." Then, her expression grew stern. "What's *she* doing here?" Jack turned to see Allison, naked in the fading darkness, frightened to speechlessness.

"Oh," chuckled Jack. "She was in bed with me." He looked up at the fiery scene again: "What happened to my house?"

"For goodness sake!" barked Lilly. "You were in your matrimonial bed with this trollop while your wife was outside watering the flowers?"

"We weren't doing anything. Besides, we kept an eye on her," Jack offered.

"Haven't you learned anything?"

Allison interjected: "In the end, the universe and everything anyone ever knew about it gets consumed in flames. It's like nothing ever happened, and nobody keeps score."

"Exactly!" Jack added, looking to Lilly for affirmation.

"That's really screwed up," Lilly said. "I truly hope you don't believe that rubbish."

"But, those are your words exactly," protested Jack.

"Didn't you see today how much people love you? How precious your life is? Didn't you feel part of a community that needs you and wants you to be a decent man? Didn't you and Martha resolve to make a new start this afternoon?"

"Yeah, we did. But, that lasted about ten minutes," Jack said.

Allison nodded in agreement. Lilly frowned.

The flames grew more intense.

"My house," Jack moaned.

"You and Martha can build a new one; it'll be like nothing ever happened," Lilly responded.

"My reputation," Jack said, hanging his head.

"Don't worry. Nobody's keeping score," Lilly assured him. "But, you have to go back. You have two great kids and there's a woman up there who would do anything for you. That's especially important for you now because you're broke."

Jack nodded meekly in acceptance. "I guess you're right," he said.

"You're broke?" Allison whispered quietly to herself. Among the gathering crowd she searched for a real man: a man who was successful, wealthy, and respected in his community.

EPILOGUE
{ LAURIE, AGAIN }

Thursday, July 3rd, 1975

It's been almost a year since the Smith house exploded and burned to the ground; a year since we were overrun with drunken off-islanders; a year since the regatta ended in a pile-up; a year since we had a near-drowning—near murder, I should say; a year since I cut my forehead in the fire truck. The island lost its appetite for excitement in a single day. Following the Fourth of July, the summer of 1974 passed quietly. Father Ivan left for a post in New Britain. Constable Nil was fired by the town council, and took a job working at a Two Guys department store in New London. There was discussion of arrest for both of them. Jack Smith spent a week or so in the hospital in Hartford with pneumonia and some bruises. But, once he recovered, the talk died down and Jack refused to press charges.

We have nothing planned for this year's Fourth. There's no picnic.

No fireworks. No white elephant sale. They're going to race sailboats, but the fleet is less than half of what it was last summer.

Riding my bicycle this morning I came upon Lilly, the Smith's elderly neighbor. She was leaning on her cane in front of the empty lot where the Smith house used to stand. I was surprised to see her return for the summer. Frankly, I was surprised that she was still alive.

"There used to be a house here," she began.

"Yes, I know, Lilly." Straddling my bike, I reached out to touch her shoulder, hoping she'd remember me. Janet, Lilly's granddaughter, came out of her cottage to join us. We shared beginning-of-summer hellos. Janet filled me in on the rumor mill:

"Liz got engaged to Larry the undertaker over Christmas."

"The undertaker? Why would she marry *him*?"

"She's desperate for a baby."

"She *must* be desperate."

"And did you hear about Mrs. Steeves' niece? She had a baby."

My jaw dropped. "Holy cow! When did that happen?"

"The first of April."

I thought about it for a moment. Nine months. She must have gotten pregnant when she was here last summer.

"Who's the father? Someone at the club?"

"She's not saying. But Mrs. Steeves and the bridge club will figure it out. And then, whoever it is—he's in big trouble."

"Have you heard anything about the Smiths?" I asked.

"They're renting this year—Jack *and* Martha," Janet said. "In fact, they arrive tomorrow."

"So, they made it through the winter together?"

Standing at the edge of the property, you might not even suspect the Smith cottage had once stood there. The lot had been cleared and filled, and was overgrown with milkweed. The garden was blooming in utter disarray.

"They're doing great, apparently."

I pondered their reconciliation. The mysteries of marriage were beyond me. Their home had blown up. How odd, it seemed to me,

that after all the hoopla, all the arguments and rumors, that Jack
and Martha should reunite. Why would they put each other through
such hardship? Wouldn't they be better off alone? I thought of Liz
marrying Larry–two people who had nothing in common. I thought
of Chloe and all the other single ladies on the island, searching for
men. I thought of the boys in the fire department, the way they vied
for my attention. Who to marry? Would I make some of the same
mistakes that everyone else seemed to make? I looked to Lily, the
oldest person on the island, for some wisdom.

"Lilly," I said, "Do you think men and women are meant to live
together?"

She looked up and squinted at me: "We're going to have an awful
lot of ants this year."